THE HOLLOW REALMS

HOLLOW KINGDOM

JORDAN ALLEN

Copyright © 2023 by Jordan Allen

Cover illustration by Lucyan Carreira

Interior illustrations by Theodoric S. Taylor

ISBN 978-1-9196192-4-8

For my beloved family.

Contents

Prologue

"We need to keep going," Kirk whispered as he helped Loretto to his feet. "I can hear more of them in the tunnels behind us."

"You need not be afraid, my friend," said Loretto with a sly grin as he adjusted himself, now upright again.

Kirk knew that Loretto was joking but now was not the time. The duo stood in the network of tunnels under the grand city of Altburg, capital of the Kingdom of Lochmeria, with only a small whirling orb of light to guide them. It circled around Kirk as he watched Loretto kick the recently slain whelp on the ground.

"He's an ugly one, isn't he?" asked Loretto.

"Well, now he's a dead one," replied Kirk gripping his blood-soaked dagger tightly. "It's thanks to me that you're not also a dead one."

Loretto frowned. He knew it was true so didn't bother to retort.

"We need to move," insisted Kirk. His patience was wearing thin. Loretto was a fine swordsman, but he was always slowing them down one way or another.

"I think my leg is bleeding, can you patch me up quickly?" asked Loretto.

Kirk sighed. He only had the divine energy to heal one more time before needing to sleep and recover, but he relented. He held his hands over Loretto's wound and focused. A soft white light emerged from Kirk's hand and the wound stitched itself up. Loretto gasped in pain, but it soon faded.

"Thank you, my friend," said Loretto genuinely. "Let's keep moving. You're right, I can definitely hear more whelps coming.

Kirk nodded and the pair crept stealthily down the tunnel. They could handle a few whelps in an open area, but if they were accosted in the narrow tunnels then they were in trouble. In fact, this is exactly how Loretto ended up on the ground in the first place.

"Wait," uttered Loretto, holding his hand up to stop Kirk. He was sure that he had heard the scraping of metal against the stone floor. He peered around the corner as Kirk dimmed his orb of light.

There was a little bit of light trickling in through gaps in the ceiling and it illuminated the room ahead. It was strewn with crates and barrels, presumably a storage area, but there was something else standing in the centre of the room.

"What do you see?" whispered Kirk as quietly as he could.

Loretto turned to face Kirk with a sly grin on his face. "It's a woman. A mighty attractive one at that."

Kirk was visibly puzzled, even in the low light. "A woman? How does she know about the Sanctuary?"

"She's dressed in robes like a priestess, but they're all white. Maybe she's here to help anybody else who escapes?"

"What should we do?"

"I'm going to go out and speak to her," said Loretto confidently. Any semblance of apprehension was now gone. "You can wait here if you're too afraid?"

"Afraid? I'm not afraid, I'm cautious," protested Kirk. "We don't even know this woman! I've never heard of a priestess in Altburg wearing entirely white robes."

"Suit yourself, Kirk," shrugged Loretto.

Kirk watched as his long-time friend strolled out into the centre of the room towards the woman. He could just about make out her features. They were soft and delicate. There was no denying her beauty, but Kirk still felt uneasy. Why was she here alone?

"Excuse me, my fair lady," said Loretto. He had a smarmy grin on his face. "Are you lost? Do you need escorting out from the tunnels?"

"Oh, by the True One!" exclaimed the lady. Her voice was soft and elegant. She turned to look at Loretto and her facial expression shifted from seemingly neutral to utter terror.

"There is no need to be afraid. My name—"

The woman turned away and ran down the tunnel, holding her robes off the ground to stop herself from tripping.

"Wait!" yelled Loretto after her.

Kirk emerged from his hiding spot and walked over to a crestfallen Loretto. "That…did not go well."

Loretto merely shook his head in confusion.

Suddenly, a female scream escaped from the tunnel that the young woman had fled down. The duo looked at each other for a moment before Loretto broke out into a sprint to chase the scream.

"Loretto! I have the light!" yelled Kirk after him. He checked his surroundings and listened carefully to try and identify any demons approaching. All seemed quiet except for Loretto's feet hitting the stone.

Kirk willed his orb to shine brighter and followed Loretto down the tunnel, albeit at a slower pace. He didn't want to trip over a loose brick and break his neck. What an unfortunate end that would be. At least a demon attack would be a fitting end, particularly considering the chaos going on in the city above.

Loretto's footsteps faded from earshot, but luckily the tunnel didn't have any junctions that weren't already blocked off in some manner. A few had collapsed and others boarded off long ago. The tunnels beneath Altburg must have been at least centuries old at this point.

"Kirk!" echoed Loretto's voice faintly from somewhere ahead. He sounded troubled. Had the woman gotten into trouble?

Kirk sped up but kept his dagger at the ready. He felt very uneasy about what may await him. There was something about that woman that Kirk couldn't put his finger on. Something unnatural.

He could sense it.

Suddenly something clicked in Kirk's head. She was a demon. He was sure of it. He wasn't a mere whelp; she was something else. She was something a lot worse. He feared for Loretto, but he couldn't abandon his friend.

Kirk turned a corner and spotted a faint light ahead. Was that the sunset? It was! There was the exit ahead, but where were Loretto and the woman? Kirk thought that he must have been wrong. Loretto surely called to alert him of the exit that the woman had led them to.

Kirk stopped dead in his tracks. No. Then why did she scream? Kirk had been following Loretto for almost a minute. It was no more than ten seconds into her running before the woman had screamed from this same tunnel.

The young cleric-in-training dimmed his light once more. Kirk looked backwards, then forwards, and began to quietly step towards the exit. Loretto had to be outside. There was nowhere else he could be.

Suddenly, a silhouette walked in front of the exit. It was the shape of a woman in robes. Loretto's heart skipped a beat and he immediately felt sick. The woman began to walk toward him. The fading sunlight was behind her, and he couldn't distinguish any of her features from this distance.

"Where is Loretto?" Kirk called out shakily. "What have you done with him?"

"It's okay, Kirk," said the woman softly. "I am here to heal your suffering."

"I am not suffering. I need no healing. Stay back!"

Kirk raised his dagger. It was still covered in blood from the whelp he had killed only minutes earlier. The woman continued to approach.

"If you will not stay back, then I will force you back," Kirk said defiantly, mustering his courage. He focused and sent a shockwave from his palm and through the air. It travelled down the tunnel and pushed the woman to the ground.

"Kirk," said the woman calmly as she floated straight upwards and back onto her feet, "I am only here to help. Let me take away the pain."

Kirk broke into an immediate sprint, sending shockwave after shockwave at the woman. He would force his way past her and escape. He would avenge the friend he now believed dead. He would survive the fall of his beloved home, Altburg.

Chapter 1

The Welcoming Party

It was a grey day in the kingdom of Lochmeria, as the days often were before spring truly set in. The lush green forests were slowly returning after another cold winter, but the path to the city of Altburg was deserted. Nobody visited Altburg anymore and anybody who was going to leave had already left months ago.

Prince Gresten's horse trotted along the road peacefully while the fair-haired prince kept an ever-vigilant watch on his surroundings from atop his steed. Danger could be behind every tree; it could come from the sky, or it could leap forth from the ground. That's what he was warned by anybody he had spoken to on his journey so far.

The prince gazed towards the peak of the castle in the not so far off distance. He hadn't seen the castle since he was two years of age, some twenty years ago. He had only the faintest of memories of his former home. He wasn't even convinced they were real memories and often wondered if the many tales he had heard from his mother and handlers had brewed the images in his mind.

Gresten's horse continued forward, blissfully unaware of her master's thoughts. She didn't have a care in the world. She was just happy to be out for a long walk. The prince gently stroked her mane as he rode along, glad of the company on the lonesome road.

The city walls slowly appeared and the trees thinned into grassland. It wasn't long before the gate itself came into view. At the very least, the archway that the gate called home did. Gresten suspected that the gates themselves hadn't been closed in a long time. Nobody wanted to go in, and for good reason, but what was inside wanted them to.

"Whoa, Hilda," said the prince as he gave a slight tug on her reins. Hilda obediently came to a stop.

Gresten paused and contemplated, looking over his left shoulder to a small field surrounded by a wooden fence. It was decision time after many hours of internal debate. Should he bring Hilda into Altburg or leave her outside? She was a lot faster than the prince, but he would be nimbler in the winding streets. She could run fast for longer than the prince, but the many stairs and alleyways could prove difficult for her. What if they were overrun by the demons that awaited them inside? Hilda wasn't in any position to defend herself against ravenous fiends.

The prince dismounted, armour clinking as he

slid onto the road below. He guided Hilda over to the field and sent her in, closing the gate behind her. It wasn't worth risking both of their lives when he may have to abandon her in Altburg before he finished his investigation.

"I will come back for you once I find out what has happened to my father," he said as he patted her side and stroked her mane. "Should I not come back, at least you're safer here."

Gresten stepped back onto the road, his hand moving to the hilt of the sword that hung from his side. He thought he may have been being overly cautious, but he reasoned that it was better to be safe than sorry. The refugees that he had spoken to in the villages along the way said that most of the demons in the city were whelps. Slow and stupid, but they could be dangerous in tight spaces or large numbers.

As the prince approached the archway in the wall that opened into the city, he was caught by surprise. It looked as though regular people were going about their business. A man was carrying a barrel across the street. A woman was dusting the road in front of a tavern door. Oddly, things seemed normal.

Gresten stepped into Altburg for the first time in two decades, but he was too focused on the people to care.

Suddenly, everybody stopped moving. Gresten did not stop walking forward as all eyes turned towards him. The eyes watching him were not normal and he was very much aware of this. The expressions of these bizarre folks were chilling. Everybody had broken out into a stretched grin and their eyes had opened so wide that their skin looked like it would tear.

Gresten gulped. From a distance, everything may have seemed calm, but the prince knew for certain now that these were no longer the citizens of Altburg. They had their faces, they may even be doing their jobs, but it was a façade. They weren't citizens serving the king, they were citizens serving Za'gerath.

The people behind Gresten began to follow him, and the people ahead of him began to move towards him. Yes, an attack was most certainly coming but, for now, they were moving slowly. He had best be quick.

Gresten moved swiftly to the left and down an alleyway. He had studied the map of the city thoroughly and had a rough idea of where to go, but there was a big difference between theory and practice. This was the true test of how well his preparation would serve him.

The alleyway behind him started to fill as the people continued to creep up towards him. He knew they were there. They knew that he knew that they were there. They were looking forward to the hunt. It didn't matter to them if he escaped for a short while. He was in their domain.

A hunched figure appeared around the corner at the far end of the alley. It was time. The prince drew his sword and charged forward. He did not have the space to slash, so he thrust the sword into the gut of the hunched figure. The blade pierced the man's side with a slick squelch, but he stood frozen in place, almost as though he was unaware that he had been attacked.

Slowly, the man turned to look at the prince and his fair flesh melted away, revealing the demon's

true face underneath. The whites of its eyes turned black, and the pupils turned to white. Its pale skin shifted into a purplish brown as though a victim of a horrible plague. Two stubs for horns erupted from the creature's forehead. Even the clothes it wore broke free from the illusion and were revealed as mere rags.

Gresten put his steel-booted foot on the whelp demon and, with a strong tug, pulled his sword from its gut, knocking the monster backwards and sending it falling to the floor.

Glancing over his shoulder, the prince could see that the citizens following him had all shed their false faces and had revealed their true forms. Demons. Every single one of them. They were moving faster towards the prince having witnessed him attacking one of their own. He couldn't fight them in such a large group, and he needed to save his energy for more dire situations.

Gresten leapt over the demon in front of him as it tried to clamber back to its feet, injured but not dead. It would surely try to follow him, but its comrades were a more pressing concern to the prince.

The path ahead forked in two directions. Where to go next? Left would lead towards the wall and right would lead further into the city. It had to be right, surely? No more time for debate, he had to move immediately.

The prince hurried through the back alleys at a brisk pace, but not quite a run. The demons were not fast, and he couldn't afford to tire himself out. He had a long way to go to reach Altburg Castle. It was the castle where he believed that he would find the king. It was there that he believed he would find his father.

The prince climbed a staircase leading out of the network of alleys, which opened up into a square. It was quiet here. The once-immaculate wooden and stone houses that populated most of the city surrounded the square. Scraps of wood, a couple of abandoned carts and a few rotten carcasses littered the area.

Gresten shuddered. He had seen the occasional dead body before, however, the smell of the decayed flesh was something that mere words from his books could not describe. Putrid was the best description he could give, but that was being generous. Gresten had killed a couple of demons in the wilderness on the way to Altburg, but they smelled distinctly different from the rotten bodies of his own kind.

He looked back down the staircase. Nothing had followed him this far. He'd best keep moving lest he be proven wrong. He didn't want to spend one more minute in this accursed city than he had to. The prince looked towards the tallest peak of the castle, which towered above the roofs of the many houses, and worked out which direction he must go.

The streets in this part of the city were as dilapidated as the square. The demons had attempted to make the entrance to Altburg look normal, but why bother once somebody had already made their way inside? They were already in the trap.

Suddenly the prince was knocked to the ground as a falling figure collided with him. A loud raspy yell broke from the mouth of his attacker. The demon's dark eyes stared at Gresten and its mouth opened wide to take a bite from his throat, but Gresten thrust his head forward into the creature's nose which made an unsettling crack as the bone broke.

The creature was dazed, and the prince threw it aside. He sprang onto his feet and stomped on the back of its head before it had the chance to rise. A nasty squelch echoed in the prince's ears as his foot crushed the demon's head, but he did not have time to focus on his disgust.

Gresten spun around to see where the demon had burst from. It had leapt from the upstairs window of a nearby building. He had expected that if an aerial attack were to come, he would hear the beatings of wings approaching.

For a moment there was silence, but that did not last. The rustling of a door handle here, the soft thud of feet on stone there. More of the demon whelps were coming. They must have been alerted by the shout of the one Gresten had just killed. The prince was not here to kill them all and reclaim his home. No, he could not waste time and energy on these beasts.

Gresten ran deeper into the city, trying to keep an eye on his surroundings as best as he could. Down this street, through that alley. No! This was the wrong way. Down this alley, through that street. Yes, this looked right. On and on he ran, trying to follow his memories of the maps.

"Agh!" exclaimed Gresten involuntarily as he turned a corner. Before the prince stood a towering, armoured figure.

The figure turned towards the prince, a long mace in its right hand, and stomped in a direct line towards him. The demon whelps from before looked gaunt and frail, however, this demon appeared much more formidable. It stood at nearly seven feet tall and wore dark metal armour. Through the slits in its helmet, its eyes glowed red while two horns protruded from gaps at the top. From a distance, you could mistake the horns for part of its helmet.

The armoured demon leaned forward and began to charge, scraping its mace along the cobblestone as it ran.

Gresten dove to the side as the demon swung the mace upwards. It was a narrow miss, but Gresten was unhurt. The demon turned to face him once again, but as Gresten climbed back to his feet his heart sank.

Demons. A dozen of the slouching whelps were shambling up the road. Gresten knew that to stand and fight would mean certain death. He was vastly outnumbered. He must run.

The armoured demon charged again and Gresten dove once more. This time, the demon's mace collided with Gresten's breastplate. The prince was winded and tried to catch his breath as the armoured demon stood over him, a towering metal pillar amongst the rubble. The demon raised its mace and swung down, but Gresten rolled sideways clumsily and clambered to his feet.

Gresten was still out of breath from being knocked to the ground, but he had to run. He dashed up the road and further towards the castle with a cluster of demons chasing him. He could hear the clank of the armoured demon's boots on the ground. It was close. He darted down a side street and began to weave his way through the streets as chaotically as he could. He had to give his enemies the slip, but he couldn't afford to attract more.

Sweat dripped from his brow as he ducked around another corner. Before too long, he paused to catch his breath. He couldn't keep running. His horse, Hilda, crossed his mind and he was now very glad that he left her outside Altburg. The distant clanking was growing closer so Gresten did the only thing he could think of. He opened the back door of the nearest house and slipped quietly inside, closing the door as softly as he could behind him.

The dusty house was quiet with no demons in sight. The prince had feared that it would be occupied by an unwelcoming resident. He crept towards the kitchen and ducked behind the table to hide from the back door and windows.

Gresten felt stupid. Here he was in a demon-infested city, hiding behind a table in an abandoned house after willingly walking through the front gates. A week ago, if you had asked him, he would have explained to you that he was going on a heroic quest. Now, he felt like an utter fool for his naivety. He had expected a challenge, yes, but he thought that his many years of studying and training on the Isle of Green wouldn't have left him in such a pathetic state.

The prince waited for a few undisturbed, but tense, minutes. He could breathe easier again after his short rest. Was now the time to continue? It was quiet, but he could not be certain that he was alone. He had to make sure.

Gresten crawled towards the window to the right of the back door and peered outside. The alley looked empty, but he would have to go out to be certain. He gently opened the door, but its old and worn hinges creaked no matter how slowly he moved it. Poking his head around the corner, he could see that the coast was clear.

Gresten pulled his map of Altburg from his pack and tried to work out where he was. He believed that he had to be in the Western quadrant of the lower residential area, but there were no clear landmarks for him to be sure. The closest place of any real note was a church with a fountain outside. If he could find that, he could know for sure where he was. If it was empty, it may be a safer place to rest.

The prince continued to work his way through the maze of wood and stone. He appreciated the haunting beauty of the finely crafted city, but he would have appreciated it more if it wasn't trying to kill him. For such a city to have fallen to such wretched creatures was a sin that the world would have to bear.

The fountain! The church! The prince could see it in the small square ahead. A wave of relief came over Gresten as he walked towards it. Looking around, he spotted a handful of straggling demons along the main road ahead. He had better get inside quickly in case they were accompanied by an armoured demon.

The church ahead was magnificent. The wooden doors were at least double the height of the prince and were bordered by ornate carvings of angelic beings. The doors were heavy and Gresten had to push hard to open them, but they slowly began to move. Once the gap was big enough, he slinked inside and closed the doors behind him hoping that the demons had not noticed him.

Prince Gresten turned and slumped against the door. After breathing a sigh of relief, he took in his surroundings. The light outside shone through stained glass windows and it painted colourful pictures on the floor. There was a statue at the far end of the hall of a flying angel with his wings unfurled and reaching one arm into the sky. Below it was a small basin that would have usually been filled with water, but Gresten couldn't know if it was from this distance.

The prince was curious, so he walked through the centre of the room, past the wooden seats and up the small steps in front of the statue. The basin did indeed have a small pool of water inside. The water looked crystal clear, perhaps it had been tended to recently? To the left of the statue was a small wooden chest filled to the brim with gold coins. Unfortunately, these were not of much use in Altburg right now and Gresten was no thief.

"Ah, a visitor," came a gentle voice from the shadows.

Gresten was startled and spun around to face the voice.

"Well, aren't you a jumpy fellow?"

"Who goes there?" asked the prince.

An old man slowly emerged from a dark corner of the hall. He was wrinkled with short grey hair and wearing long robes of red and gold. Gresten strained his eyes and could see that there was a small door beside the man.

"Say," said the old man, "let me see your face."

Gresten took a step back and moved his hand to his sword.

"There will be no need for such extreme measures, my son. Do I look dangerous? Surely not."

"Forgive me," said Gresten uneasily, "but I'm sure you can understand my apprehension considering the disorder to be found in this once fine city. Who would live here if they were not of ill intent?"

The man sighed. "That is fair. You could say that things have taken a turn for the worse over the last few months, but I assure you that I have no ill intent towards you."

Gresten eased ever so slightly. He couldn't explain why, but he believed the old man, who resumed his approach.

"Your face, my son. It's very familiar to me. You look like the lost prince of this city. Would you happen to be Prince Germund Lochmeria?"

"I'm afraid you're mistaken, sir. I am his brother, Prince Gresten Lochmeria."

"Ah, so you're not the lost prince. You're the long-lost prince. I haven't heard your name uttered in quite some time. I was led to believe that you and your mother were both dead."

"My mother is dead, but I am still alive."

"I see. I know about your father's fate, I'm sad to say, but what of your twin?"

Gresten paused for a moment at the utterance of his father before responding. "I have not seen Germund for twenty years. My last letter from him was seven years ago, just before I sent word to him about our mother's death. It was the last time that I heard from either him or our father."

"I am sorry to hear that. I will say a prayer to the True One. Maybe he will tell me if your mother's soul reached the Inner World."

"I'm sure she would appreciate that. As would

I."

"Come, let us sit and you can tell me why you're here in Altburg. I do not doubt that we have a lot to discuss."

The man slowly walked back to his room and beckoned for Gresten to follow him.

"What is your name, sir?" asked Gresten before moving.

"I am Saint Rudolph, young prince. Welcome home."

Chapter 2

The Last Saint of Altburg

Gresten fell to his knees and dropped into a deep bow before Saint Rudolph. He had been taught by his handlers that high ranking priests were on par with most royalty, but saints were esteemed beyond all royalty save for the monarch. He could not believe the disrespect he had shown to a Saint of the True One, whether he had known his identity or not.

"Revered Saint Rudolph, I did not know of your prestige. Forgive me."

"How could you have known, young prince? You are forgiven. An accidental sin is much more easily washed away than a known sin."

Saint Rudolph turned back towards his room. The prince climbed back to his feet, thoroughly embarrassed, and followed.

The back room that Saint Rudolph led the

prince to was dignified but considerably less majestic than the main hall. It was a small study lined with wooden bookshelves packed with tomes and scrolls. The stone floor was well polished, in stark contrast with the floor of the house that Gresten had hidden in earlier.

Saint Rudolph gestured towards a small chair by a lit fireplace and Gresten sat down.

"Pardon me, your reverence," began Gresten, "but won't the demons outside see the smoke?"

"Yes, I'm sure they will," said Saint Rudolph as he moved a log closer to the centre of the fire, "but they will not get in. This church will not let a demon enter while I'm alive."

The prince felt a wave of relief sweep over him. He was safe here under the protection of the True One and his saint.

"Now tell me, Prince Gresten Lochmeria," said Saint Rudolph as he also sat down, "why did you come to Altburg?"

"I came to find out what happened to my father, your reverence. Word reached the Isle of Green about Za'gerath so I knew that I must come. We have long been hearing of the rise of the demons on mainland Lochmeria, but a demon ruling as though he were king is a matter of great concern to me. If you would be so kind, I would appreciate it if you could tell me what you know."

"Where should I begin?" asked Saint Rudolph earnestly.

"Please begin when the demons first began appearing in numbers throughout Lochmeria, your reverence."

Saint Rudolph stared into the fire and sighed. "It first started at the same time as the plague began to ease nineteen years ago. As Altburg began to rebuild, demon sightings became more and more common. Once or twice a year turned into once or twice a month. Altburg remained largely unharmed until maybe ten years ago. In fact, the city was even more prosperous then than it was before the plague decimated our lands."

Gresten had always wondered why his father had sent he and his mother away during the plague yet had never asked for them to come back once the plague had passed. His father had ordered them explicitly to remain on the Isle of Green.

"Around six months ago," Saint Rudolph continued, "the heaviest wave of demon attacks began in the city. Nobody knew where the demons themselves were coming from. Some appeared as if out of thin air, others swore that the demons were possessing the bodies of the citizens. People brought their loved ones to me as soon as they started showing signs of possession and I purged many a demon, as did my fellow clergymen across the city. I hadn't seen as many dead since the plague itself.

"Seemingly out of nowhere, the king's advisors sent word that he was no longer to be called King Gerath Lochmeria. He was now officially to be addressed as King Za'gerath."

"You said that it was seemingly out of nowhere?"

"Yes. Most people didn't expect it, however, word travels faster through the church than it does through the streets. The clerics and priests in the castle were sent away years ago, but there are still devout followers of the True One in the castle and they kept me abreast of what was happening. The

True One sent me a sign and he confirmed my fear that the king himself was possessed."

The prince was dismayed. "I feared that this may be the case as soon as I heard my father was to be known as Za'gerath. Your reverence, do you know how this could have happened?"

"Oftentimes, it involves a deal with a powerful demon. Once the demon fulfils its end, it collects what was promised to it. There have been large scale demon attacks and possessions throughout thousands of years of history, but this is unlike anything I know of. What was the deal itself? I cannot say for I do not know."

"How would I learn this? Any direction you can give me would be much appreciated, your reverence. I have much gold that I can donate if it is still of use to you? I fear that it may not be, but if there is another way to repay you, I will do that also."

"Do not worry, young prince. I am well taken care of here. The True One provides. If you want to find out what happened to your father, then I'm afraid you must find him for yourself. The only other person who may know is your brother, Prince Germund."

"Saint Rudolph, you said my brother was the lost prince and that I was the long-lost prince. What happened to him?"

"That, I'm afraid, I also do not know," said Saint Rudolph. "There has been a disturbing number of missing royal family members throughout the Outer World. Did you hear about King Elrich's disappearance in Kalmere a few decades ago?"

"As great a mystery as that is, Saint Rudolph, it is not one I can focus on."

"Quite right," said the saint as he rose to his feet. "Come, I will fetch you some bread and you can rest here for the evening. I will give you a blessing in the morning and you can make your way to the castle."

Prince Gresten stood up. "I'm surprised you're not going to try and stop me, your reverence."

Saint Rudolph chuckled. "I know that you would not, even if I had any desire to stop you. You may be brave, or you simply may be foolish, but sometimes it takes foolish optimism to push a man to action."

"I am a capable warrior, but it is true that I am sheltered. Foolish optimism may be the best way to describe my current state of mind, but to not try and learn the truth would be shameful. I must know the full story of my father's fate and, if I can find it, my brother's also. For that, I am less hopeful."

"Always maintain hope, Prince Gresten. Look at my current situation. I survive in a city of demons, yet none of them can harm me. A seemingly impossible situation, but divine will sees that it is so."

Saint Rudolph and Prince Gresten continued to talk until sunset before Saint Rudolph retired to his quarters. The prince lay on the floor using his pack as a pillow and his cloak as a blanket. Thoughts raced around his mind, but his exhaustion from the day caught up to him quickly.

*

"Saint Rudolph! I need your help!" yelled a gruff voice, bursting through a back door into the church.

"Yes, Master Wagner. I am here," called Saint Rudolph from the main hall.

Prince Gresten put his morning bread down and hurried into the main hall to see what the commotion was. A brown-haired man who looked to be in his mid-30s was sitting on the steps at the front of the hall clutching his side. Blood was seeping through the rags he tied around his wound. Saint Rudolph was kneeling beside him about to remove the rags.

"Young prince," said Saint Rudolph, "please hold Master Wagner still."

"That will not be necessary, your reverence," said Wagner.

"I know what I am doing, Master Wagner. Prince, if you please."

Gresten hurried over to Wagner and pinned him down while Saint Rudolph removed the bandages. The saint laid his on Wagner's wound and a soft white light emerged. Gresten knew this spell, Healing Hands, well. He and his training partners suffered many an injury that the Isle of Green priests had taken care of.

Before Gresten's eyes, Wagner's wound began to stitch itself back together while the man winced from the pain. The wound was deep, and Wagner began to recoil, but the prince held him still.

Saint Rudolph stood up and sat on the nearest bench. Wagner and Gresten both arose, Wagner wiping the sweat from his brow with his sleeve.

"Thank you, Saint Rudolph." said Wagner taking a deep bow, "As ever, I'm in your debt, your reverence."

"You are welcome, my son. May the True One be with you."

"What happened?" asked Gresten more bluntly than he intended.

"Who are you? Prince?" asked Wagner with a frown.

"My name is Prince Gresten Lochmeria. I have come to find out the truth about what happened to my father."

Wagner's frown turned into a smile, and he began to laugh. "I thought you were dead, your highness. You have picked a strange time to return to Altburg."

"It is precisely because of the strange time that I have returned."

Saint Rudolph cleared his throat and looked at Wagner pointedly.

"Forgive me, my prince," said Wagner as he took another bow. "I should not be so discourteous. To answer your question, I was attacked by a blackguard. The big, armoured demons that patrol the streets. I'm not one for heavy armour because I want to be quick, but clearly, I am not fast enough."

"You will stay here and rest awhile, Master Wagner," Saint Rudolph interjected. "I trust that you have brought what I requested?"

"Yes, your reverence," replied Wagner. "Seven fish and a pound of salt. I caught the fish myself and Eburhard, the bounty hunter, helped me locate the salt. I hope that is enough."

"More than enough, thank you. I will prepare the fire."

Saint Rudolph returned to his room leaving

Gresten and Wagner in the main hall.

"Master Wagner," began the prince. "What sort of dangers are there on the way to the castle? Have you ever made it inside?"

Wagner grimaced. "I avoid that place like the plague, your highness. Nobody ever makes it past the bridge without facing off against the guardian of the bridge. He's five times your size and ten times as powerful."

"What would it take to get past him?"

"Speed, magic, and luck. Do you have any of those, Prince Gresten?"

Gresten paused for a moment to think. "If I recall correctly, the bridge is half a mile long. If something can distract him long enough for me to get to the other—"

"With all due respect, your highness. I'm not doing it."

"I wasn't asking you to, Master Wagner. I was merely thinking aloud. You are free to do whatever it is that you do around Altburg. What is it that you do?"

"Me?" chuckled Wagner. "I find what's been left behind, and I help keep Saint Rudolph fed and watered. There are still a few folks lingering in Altburg, some of us looking for treasure and others looking for trouble. It's not a bad life. This broken world makes more sense to me than it did when it was whole. I don't see myself leaving anytime soon. As for you, your highness, I suggest you leave this accursed city. I say this with respect and concern for your wellbeing."

Wagner gave a small bow to the prince as he left the hall to join Saint Rudolph, leaving Gresten alone.

The awe-inspiring statue of the angel towered over Gresten who knelt before it. He did not care what Wagner said or how dangerous things may be. It was his duty as the prince of this kingdom to spread the truth of what happened to the king. Gresten did not believe his father would make a deal with a demon for no good reason.

Gresten bowed his head and prayed. "O True One, grandmaster of the Inner World. Let strength be granted to me, so that I may know the truth. As true as your name, so true must be my family legacy. I ask this of thee as a humble servant."

*

"Focus all of the energy within your soul, Prince," said Saint Rudolph from a seat in the main hall.

Gresten raised his two hands together, closed his eyes and said a short but silent prayer. He willed divine energy to flow from his hands.

"Nothing is happening," said Wagner. "I don't think you're doing it right, your highness."

"It would help if you would allow me to concentrate," said Gresten.

"That will do, Wagner," said Saint Rudolph. "Prince. I suspect that you're trying too hard to let the spell come from your mind, not from your soul. You don't need to think the prayer, you need to feel the prayer. Your mind should be blank, your soul should be praying. That is the essence of the Push spell. Please, try again."

Prince Gresten took a deep breath and cleared

his mind. He tried to pray but found the words creeping into his head rather than feeling the meaning behind them. He cleared his mind once again and focused. The parchment before him blew off the table and onto the floor.

Saint Rudolph clapped his hands gently, but enthusiastically, while Wagner looked confused.

"Are you sure that was it?" asked Wagner. "It's draughty in here, it may have been the wind. Should I put it back on the table and he can try again?"

"No," said the saint, "that was the spell. I know this to be true. That was a good first effort, Prince."

"Thank you, Saint Rudolph, "said Gresten. "I was not allowed to train in any of the schools of magic. My handlers would only allow physical combat training. I asked many times, but even my mother told me that I could not."

Saint Rudolph didn't speak immediately. "It is customary for royal family members to focus on military tactics and combat while dedicated priests and mages serve in the military. There is no military left to lead so I deem it appropriate to teach you divine magic. I assure you that you are not the first in your line to train in this way. I also believe that the fact that you were able to create even a small force means that you are divinely blessed. Your wisdom must be great."

Gresten was eased. He feared that he was breaching ancient customs, but he trusted that Saint Rudolph was being honest with him.

"Try again," said Saint Rudolph, "but you may only have a small handful of divine energy left. It exhausts more quickly for the inexperienced than those who have trained their spirit for as long as I have. You can always try again tomorrow if you find that you do not have the strength."

The prince continued to practise casting his spell for the next hour, but true to Saint Rudolph's prediction, he ran out of steam quite quickly. It was good progress, but Gresten didn't believe that it would do much more than blow off a whelp's hat without more training. He would be departing in the morning to try and reach the castle.

The three men enjoyed a simple supper of bread and fish, sharing a few stories from their lives. Gresten talked of his life on the Isle of Green, Saint Rudolph spoke of his love for his congregation that he sorely missed, and Wagner told tales of his many brushes with death in the city. It was an evening enjoyed by all and Gresten felt ready to face the challenges that he knew awaited him the next morning.

Chapter 3

Metal and Stone

"I'm too old and slow to be able to outpace the Bridge Guardian," said Saint Rudolph, "but you may be able to do it. That may, however, also be naïve optimism on my part, dear prince. I have not as much as seen him, only heard the tales from the stragglers who visit this church."

"I can only try, your reverence," said Gresten. "I appreciate your hospitality, Saint Rudolph. You have my most sincere gratitude."

"If you have need of my prayers or healing from the divine, I will be here. I do not know how long you will remain in Altburg, my prince, but do not forget to train your magic."

Wagner walked up to the prince and bowed. "I wish you the best of luck, your highness. If I may offer one piece of advice, it is to not attract the Bridge Guardian's attention unless you absolutely must."

"Thank you, Master Wagner," said Gresten.

Gresten gave both Saint Rudolph and Wagner a courteous nod before walking down the steps into the square. The air had a chill to it this morning, but the sky was clear. Gresten glanced around the streets and could see a couple of whelps skulking around, but they had yet to notice him.

The prince seized the opportunity to push forward undisturbed, keeping low behind the rubble littering the streets. A whelp was banging its head against a door as though in a daze. While it was distracted, Gresten snuck up behind it and jammed his knife into the side of its skull. The whelp slinked to the ground dead and the street ahead was now clear, but the prince would hesitate to call it safe.

He kept to the shadows cast by the buildings on the left side of the street and tried to make his way to the bridge. He knew that it wasn't too dangerous at this moment in time, but he didn't want to attract any unnecessary attention. His initial attempt at infiltrating the city made it very clear to him that a stealthy approach would be his best bet if he wanted to reach the castle alive.

Gresten was forced to kill a handful of whelps on his way through the streets and he was lucky enough not to have come face to face with another blackguard or any hordes. He believed this to be a sign from the True One. Saint Rudolph's blessing was serving him well.

There it was; it was the bridge. The prince walked cautiously, looking from side to side to ensure he was alone, but before he could get close an armoured figure stepped out from behind a pillar. Gresten stopped and drew his sword, ready to face off against the blackguard. This would only be a minor setback.

"Who goes there?" asked the figure.

Gresten was taken aback. He had never heard a demon speak his language before.

"I asked you a question, lad," stated the figure sternly.

"Why does my reason for being here interest you, demon?" asked the prince.

"I am no demon. I am simply a man looking to cross a bridge. If you do not get in my way, then we are not enemies."

"Well, then it would seem that we have a common goal."

The figure walked towards Gresten, and it became clear that he was no blackguard. He was closer in height to Gresten and lacked the distinctive horns that the majority of demons possessed. The man's armour, however, was a similarly dark metal and his face was concealed by the grill of his helmet. He put his sword away as he came within feet of Gresten.

"You still haven't told me your name, lad," said the man.

"My name is Gresten," said the prince. He started to wonder if telling strangers his identity was a good idea. "And you?"

"Ah, just like the dead prince. My name is Reinhold. What is it you seek from the castle? If it's riches you're after, then might I suggest plundering the thousands of other buildings in Altburg?"

Gresten had to think of a lie fast. "I seek a family heirloom that was on my brother when he died. He served as one of the guards posted at the castle. It would please my mother greatly to see it returned."

"You would risk your life for an heirloom?"

"Yes."

"Fair enough. That is your business, friend. Might I propose a temporary alliance until we reach the castle?"

"That would be most welcome," said Gresten earnestly. "I thought that I may have to rely mostly on luck to get past the Bridge Guardian."

"Ah, you know of him already. Well, that settles it."

"Do you have a plan?"

"I do," said Reinhold. "The Bridge Guardian is a giant encased in stone armour. His weakness is his joints, much like anyone wearing armour. His normal skin is tough and looks like stone, but it is not stone. If one of us can serve as bait, the other can strike at his heels. I believe that it would be our best shot. If we can't knock him off of the bridge, at least we'll be able to able to prevent him from chasing us."

"Am I to serve as the bait?" asked Gresten suspiciously.

Reinhold let out a guttural laugh. "No, my friend. I will do that. You would have no assurance that I wouldn't abandon you otherwise, would you?"

"That is fair. Lead the way, Master Reinhold."

The duo walked towards the bridge. The entrance was a stone archway adorned with magnificent stone carvings of kings, queens, and depictions of notable scenes from Lochmerian history. Gresten recognised the image of a man beheading a wyvern as the tale of Sir Strom defending Castle Altburg from wyverns sent by the sorcerer Tobaj.

The archway led to the bridge. It was about fifty feet wide and paved with once-pristine grey bricks that were now plagued with moss and weeds after not being tended to for so long. Both sides of the bridge were lined with walls that only reached Gresten's waist. He glanced over and down into the river far below. The Runder River ran across most of Lochmeria and straight through Altburg. The city itself was first founded millennia ago because of the fish that inhabited the river. To think that it had become a sprawling monument to the Lochmerians after so long only for it to fall in a few years was tragic.

"Have you ever been here before?" asked Reinhold.

"Not in a long time, no," replied Gresten.

"Look up ahead, Master Gresten."

Gresten turned towards the castle ahead. His eyes panned down from the top spire to the archway in the distance. Halfway across the bridge, Gresten could see a towering figure that was almost as wide as the bridge itself. The Bridge Guardian.

"That's him?" asked Gresten.

"That's him. He may have seen us; he may not have. Either way, he won't move until we get closer."

Reinhold led the way and Gresten followed very closely behind. Gresten couldn't see how anything would sneak up on them, but he continually kept an eye on his surroundings. Had the city made him paranoid already? Perhaps that was for the best if he wanted to remain alive.

As the duo approached the Bridge Guardian, Gresten could see him more clearly. Wagner was right in saying that the Bridge Guardian was much taller than the prince. He resembled a large golem with armour that was hard to distinguish from his body. The armour was made of a rough grey stone and his hands were shaped like giant hammers. Being crushed under one of those hammers would surely be deadly so losing sight of the guardian's hands could be a fatal mistake.

When the duo was within a hundred yards of the Bridge Guardian he finally stirred. Both men drew their swords and Reinhold readied his shield. The Bridge Guardian was striding towards them, and he was closing in fast even at his walking pace.

"When I clash with him, you run behind him and aim for the tendons at the back of the feet. Do you understand?" asked Reinhold.

"Yes," said Gresten. He would be lying if he said he was ready, but he knew that this was his duty. There was no turning back now.

"Good," said Reinhold. "Then let us waste no time."

Reinhold ran towards the Bridge Guardian, his shield raised. The Bridge Guardian drew back his gigantic hammer fist and swung it through the air, knocking Reinhold flat on his back. Gresten had already started to charge before Reinhold fell.

The Bridge Guardian raised another fist ready to crush Reinhold, but Gresten's mad dash between his legs distracted the behemoth. As Gresten raised his sword to slash the heel of the stone-coated colossus, he leapt backwards in the direction of the castle and Gresten simply slashed the air.

"He's faster and more intelligent than I anticipated," called Reinhold as he climbed to his feet. "No matter. We must flank him."

The Bridge Guardian squatted low. He raised both fists and charged forward. The large demon was determined to barrel through both men, who immediately scurried for the side of the bridge to avoid being flattened. After the near miss, the Bridge Guardian turned to look at Reinhold.

Reinhold raised his weapon and stabbed the giant in the eye, and it stood up in pain. If it could have screamed in agony, it would have, but it lacked the mouth to utter as much as a whisper. The Bridge Guardian flailed for a moment and Gresten seized the opportunity to attack it again. He slashed at the colossus's heel, but the beast barely flinched and extracted the sword from his eye, discarding it like a toothpick.

Reinhold retreated to retrieve his sword, his shield still raised. The Bridge Guardian ignored Gresten attacking his foot and swung a mighty fist, colliding with Reinhold's shield. With a large clang, the shield soared into the air and the man was flung over the edge of the bridge.

Gresten ran to the edge of the bridge and watched in horror as Reinhold's body fell over two hundred feet into the river below, followed by his rapidly spinning shield.

The Bridge Guardian turned to Gresten, who gazed up at it for a moment before sprinting as fast as he could towards the castle. He was determined to not share the fate of his ally, cowardly as this move may have been. Gresten could hear the stomping of the beast behind him, and he knew that it was going to catch him, but still, he ran.

As Gresten grew ever closer to the end of the bridge, the stomping slowed and eventually stopped. He turned to look at the Bridge Guardian who simply stared at him, standing completely still. Why did it stop?

Before Gresten had a chance to think about it, he had his answer. He was knocked to the ground by a pair of fat demons in leather armour, brandishing chains. One of the demons broke into a toothy grin before raising a small club and knocking Gresten out cold.

*

Gresten opened his eyes. He looked around and saw that he was in a small stone room with three brick walls surrounding him along with a division of bars and a metal door, made from similar bars, that separated him from a corridor. There was a small window above him from which the moonlight shone through. It illuminated his prison cell slightly more than the glowing orange from the torches in the hallway.

The prince felt foolish. It was obvious to him now that there would be more guards outside the gates to the castle. Why didn't this occur to him before? A costly mistake and one he would not repeat, should he find a way to freedom.

He slowly climbed to his feet. There was nothing else in his cell except for a small wooden bucket in the corner. Was the bucket a kindness from the demons or a holdover from before they were here? He supposed it didn't matter because he did not want to stay for long. The main question now plaguing his mind was how he would escape this new predicament.

Gresten, now unarmoured and unarmed, walked over to the window and looked outside. He was still in Altburg, but he knew that he wasn't in the main districts of the city. He could see the silhouette of the castle towers and realised that he was on the central island overlooking the river. He was indeed across the bridge, but very much blocked from the castle.

The prince slumped down, despondent. He looked over at his bucket and raised his hands to try and force it to move with his magic. It shook ever so slightly, but no more.

"Casting spells, are we?" came a voice from outside the cell. "You'd better not let them catch you doing that."

Gresten walked over to his bars and looked outside. There was a man with long scraggly brown hair and a rough beard staring at him from a cell across the hall. The man was faintly illuminated by the flickering torches. They cast shadows on his face that made him look considerably older than he probably was.

"Who are you?" asked Gresten.

"My name is Sir Brand of Lochmeria," he replied.

"Sir Brand Lochmeria?"

"Of Lochmeria. No, I am not a member of the royal family. Merely a humble knight of a once-great kingdom, now a filthy prisoner locked up in a city that I once called home."

Gresten wasn't quite sure what to ask Sir Brand as his head was still throbbing from the beating, courtesy of the fat demon.

"You're not one for words, are you?" asked Sir Brand.

Gresten let out a slight chuckle. "What is there to say? It seems as though we're both trapped in here with no way out."

"I could probably get out if I wanted to."

"You could?"

"I've been here since the city fell half a year ago. I don't have any reason to leave, so I choose to remain."

"That sounds awfully defeatist of you."

"That's because Lochmeria has been defeated. Altburg has fallen, so too the monarchy. What use would I be outside these walls?"

Gresten's mood was not improved by the pessimism emanating from Sir Brand.

"Altburg may have fallen," said Gresten conceding that particular point, "but I came from outside the city. Most of the kingdom is still whole, albeit there is no shortage of suffering. The Isle of Green, small as it may be, is prospering and peaceful even to this date. No demons have reached its shores."

"Yet," said Sir Brand, raising his eyebrows. "They will eventually. It is only a matter of time. As goes Altburg, so goes the rest of Lochmeria. It's inevitable."

"You have so little hope and faith left, Sir Brand?"

"So little? I have zero, stranger. Absolutely zero."

"If you can truly escape, tell me how."

"Oh, that's very simple. Grab a guard, knock him out, take his keys and fight your way through.

They're stupid buggers, that's for sure."

"In what way is that simple, Sir Brand?"

"I'm a very capable fighter, I assure you. Even without any weapons to speak of. Evidently, your magical skills aren't going to do you any favours when you can't even tip over a bucket."

"I may yet lack the ability to perform even the most basic of divine spells but put a sword in my hand and I am also a capable fighter."

"If you say so," said Sir Brand, shrugging nonchalantly. He walked to the back of his cell and lay down on the ground. "I'm going to sleep. We can talk more in the morning if it suits you. I grow weary of banging my head against the brick wall of your words. The wardens will bring you your food once per day. Savour it because it's all you will get. Use your bucket sparingly as they'll only empty it once a fortnight. I recommend trying to tip it through the window bars after each...erm, deposit."

Prince Gresten was thoroughly unimpressed by this supposed knight of the kingdom. Perhaps if Sir Brand knew that a royal family member was still alive it would help his attitude, but Gresten thought that the man was far too lost in his own misery to care.

The prince stood at the far end of his cell with his hands raised. He conjured up all of the willpower in his soul to try and knock the bucket over. If he was going to escape, then he would need to use the only weapon he had left. Gresten was convinced that the True One had steered him towards Saint Rudolph for a reason and that this was the reason. He was always fated to be locked in this cell and the saint had given him his key.

An hour later, the prince finally managed to knock over his bucket. He was exhausted and sank onto the floor. He was resolute that he would not die in this cell. One way or another, he would be free.

Chapter 4

Until Sunrise

Three weeks had passed and true to what Sir Brand had said, the excrement bucket had only been emptied once. Gresten had grown used to hunger and was indeed savouring his daily meal of a single small loaf and a large cup of water. It was a meagre meal, but he longed for the next each time he finished.

"Why are we being kept alive?" Gresten asked Sir Brand.

"Humiliation," said Sir Brand nonchalantly. "It's the only reason that I can think of."

"This doesn't bother you?"

"I'm just grateful that they've never defiled me at this point, Pama."

Gresten had given Sir Brand a fake name. He was concerned that if the demons had heard his real name uttered then he would no longer be kept alive.

"If I can escape, will you come with me?" asked Gresten checking the corridor for patrolling guards.

"No," said Sir Brand. "I've told you to stop asking me that. I will provide you with no help because then I will be killed. And I do not want to be killed."

"What do you even live for?"

Sir Brand hesitated for a moment before answering the question. "I live because I fear death. Don't you?"

"Routine humiliation and demonisation are fates worse than death, Sir Brand. If my soul is not fit to travel to the Inner World, then so be it."

"This Outer World has become so hollow to me that I suspect the Inner World is also hollow."

"One day, Sir Brand, you will see. I swear to you, not all is lost."

"One day, Pama, you may be able to knock over your bucket on the first try. I swear to you, it will happen."

Gresten raised his hands in the direction of his bucket and focused. He breathed deep and the spell flowed from his palms, knocking the empty bucket to the floor.

"Well," said Sir Brand, "you've certainly improved. Now be sure to tell me when knocking over buckets lets you defeat the army of wardens standing between you and freedom."

Three weeks of doom and gloom emanating from Sir Brand had only strengthened Gresten's resolve. It wasn't pleasant to listen to, but he used the negativity as fuel. He walked over to his window and stared out as the setting sun fell behind the castle. It was quite beautiful to see, even knowing that the city was a husk. Even the demons could not take away the beauty of sun and shadow.

As Gresten stared, he heard a fat warden stomping up the corridor. He had a grim snarl on his hideous, boil-covered face as he carried a sack of bread with him. He threw a small loaf through the bars to Gresten and another to Sir Brand. He set a cup on the floor at each of their doors and poured water from a waterskin into it.

"Thank you," said Gresten out of instinct. He had a habit of being well-mannered to the demons even knowing that it was pointless. It was hard to shake.

The demon didn't even turn to look at him. It never did. They never seemed to as much as acknowledge the existence of prisoners, not counting the mealtime deliveries.

"Can they talk?" asked Gresten as the demon stomped onwards to deliver meals to other prisoners. He had always assumed that demons could talk, but he had never heard anything outside of shouts and grunts.

"Some of them can, yes," answered Sir Brand. "A warden has only ever spoken to me once. He told me to be silent when I first arrived here. I was putting up quite the struggle and I think that if I didn't comply, they'd have probably killed me. They have very deep voices that warble as though three people are speaking in unison. It's one of those things that you need to hear for yourself for it to truly make sense."

Gresten and Sir Brand ate their meals in silence and then Gresten returned to training his spellcasting. He thought it was an interesting turn of fate that he chose not to remain with Saint Rudolph for longer, yet here he was stuck in one place for almost a month. Fate has a funny way of telling you that you should have taken good advice when it was given to you.

Before long, the sun had set, and the crescent moon was creeping out from behind the wispy clouds. Gresten lay against the wall of his cell staring out at the moon, oddly at peace. Sir Brand's snores were a rather unfitting backdrop for the otherwise serene view from the window. Gresten closed his eyes for what he had only intended to be a moment and drifted off.

"Now is not the time to be sleeping," came an ever-so-slightly muffled voice.

Gresten jolted awake and looked around. There was nobody there.

"Window," said the voice, barely louder than a whisper.

Gresten looked up and saw a dark shadow at his window. He rose and walked over, fearful but curious. The shadow was a man. He was wearing a brown wooden mask with his hood pulled up to cover his hair. The mask was carved to look like a man's face except for a pair of tusks that rose out from the mouth. The man's entire face was obscured, but Gresten could faintly see his blue eyes through the eyeholes.

"How did you get up here?" said a flabbergasted prince.

"I climb well," said the man dismissively, "but now is not the time for tales of my abilities. You are going to be executed in the morning, Prince Gresten. You must leave and you must leave

tonight."

"Executed? How do they know who I am?" asked Gresten. "How do you know who I am?"

"We can speak once we're not separated by bars. You must escape from this prison. You have until sunrise."

"How?" said Gresten.

"Work it out. I cannot get you out of this cell, but if you can set yourself free then I can guide you from outside. Once you're loose, make your way downstairs to the kitchens. That's the nearest place I can reach without breaking my neck."

The man began climbing downwards.

"What is your name?" asked Gresten.

"Hurm," said the man. He continued to climb downwards, but Gresten couldn't see what he was grabbing onto to do so. It was not long before he was out of sight, as though he had never been there.

Gresten looked around at the cell he had reluctantly called his own. He had no idea how to get out of it before morning. The Push spell wasn't exactly meant for unlocking doors. It simply pushed things. Suddenly, Gresten felt an idea strike him like a bolt of lightning.

"Sir Brand," called Gresten, hoping he didn't alert the wardens yet.

"Ugh," said Sir Brand as he stirred from his slumber.

"Sir Brand!" called Gresten slightly louder.

"What? What do you want, Pama?" replied the scruffy knight.

"I need your help urgently," said Gresten, lowering his voice. "I need to get out of here tonight."

"What? Tonight?"

"A man climbed up to my window and told me that I'll be executed tomorrow morning. I have until sunrise."

"You were dreaming, Pama. Nobody climbed up to your window. That's a ridiculous notion and I want no part of it."

Sir Brand lay back down and rolled over. Gresten's anger grew, but he suddenly thought of another plan. It was rash, but he had to try.

"AGH!" shouted the prince at the top of his lungs.

"What in Za was that? Have you gone mad, Pama?" asked Sir Brand in shock as he climbed to his feet.

"My name is not Pama, Sir Brand," said Gresten hurriedly. "My name is Prince Gresten Lochmeria, and you are one of my subjects. You will help me escape this cell."

Sir Brand simply stared in shock as stomping footsteps approached quickly.

A warden rounded the corner and marched up towards Gresten's cell. Gresten could see the keys hanging from the belt that was partially covered by a thick roll of fat. Gresten raised his hands and quickly cast his spell. A powerful force erupted from his palms, knocking the warden backwards and onto the floor.

The warden was dazed and tried to stand up, but Sir Brand put an arm around its neck and pulled. Sir Brand used his other hand to fumble for the keys as the warden pummelled at the knight's arm on its neck.

"Catch," called Sir Brand as he threw the keys to Gresten.

Gresten reached his arm through the bars and caught the keys. He quickly unlocked the door and ran to Sir Brand's aid. The prince delivered relentless kicks to the head of the fat demon as Sir Brand continued to restrain it. It didn't take too many kicks for the demon's skull to cave in and its brains splatter across the bars. Shoving the demon aside, Gresten opened Sir Brand's cell door.

"Thank you," said Gresten sincerely.

"Was it true?" asked the knight. "Are you who you say you are?"

"Yes. I am one of the twin princes."

"Are you here to put an end to Za'gerath and save our kingdom? Dare I hope?"

"Yes," lied Gresten. "I will see Altburg freed from the clutches of these demons. All is *not* lost, Sir Brand."

More loud stomps approached as the two Lochmerians ran into the hallway.

"Go," demanded Sir Brand, picking up a torch from the wall and a baton from the dead warden.

"Come with me, Sir Brand," urged Gresten.

"I will be right behind you, my prince," said the knight defiantly. "If I do not follow, then don't remember me as a despondent coward."

"Thank you, Sir Brand."

"Go!"

Gresten ran down the hall in the opposite direction of the stomping. He wasn't sure which way the nearest staircase was, but away from the wardens seemed like a good place to start. As he ran, Gresten watched as other prisoners, both human and demon stared out at him. He didn't have time to question what the demons were doing there, but he tossed the keys into one of the cells containing a man. There was no time to unlock each himself so he had to trust the man would do the right thing.

A staircase! Gresten began to walk down the stairs, but suddenly a fat figure emerged below. It was a warden. It yelled with anger and charged up the stairs, but Gresten held out his hands and cast his Push spell. The warden was flung backwards and down the stairs, cracking its head on the wall. Gresten charged down and grabbed his club. He pummelled the demon until its skull was as crushed as the last one.

Gresten straightened up and let out a grunt. It was a satisfying rush taking out these beasts knowing what they had done to his home. He didn't even feel tired or hungry anymore. The prince was running solely on adrenaline and a burning desire to escape.

Wielding the filthy wooden club, the prince ran through the archway at the bottom of the staircase and looked around. This hallway didn't have any cells, but it had plenty of rooms. Gresten hurriedly put his head into each as he passed, hoping for something that would aid his escape.

The armoury. Excellent! Gresten quickly tossed open each trunk and chest, seeking his armour. He found it in the fifth one he checked and haphazardly stashed it in one of the empty sacks. There was no time to stop to put on the armour, so Gresten ran from the room. The prince would have to make do with the baton for now, for his sword and knife were nowhere to be found.

Gresten continued to look through the rooms hoping to find the kitchen, but to no avail. He could hear a stomping coming from the stairs behind him and he knew that the wardens had gotten past Sir Brand.

"Here!" yelled a voice from a room at the end of the hall.

Gresten could see Hurm's mask in a narrow window through an open doorway. He ran to his newfound guide hoping there wouldn't be much further to go.

"I wasn't certain that you would succeed," said Hurm.

"I must," replied Gresten.

"Indeed. We have no time to waste. I can't squeeze through this window so all I can offer is directions."

"A better weapon than this brutish club would be most appreciated."

"I will see what I can do, but no more chatter. The bottom floor is well guarded by wardens, so the front door is out of bounds. You need to go leave this room, go left and find the next staircase downwards. Once you're there, there is a window at the far end of the corridor. It should be just big enough for you to squeeze through."

"You want me to jump from the window? What's below me?"

"The Runder. You have to jump into the river. Swim ashore at the eastern side and I will meet you there. Now go. I can see them coming down the corridor behind you."

With that, Hurm dropped out of sight. Gresten turned and also saw the wardens marching down the corridor. He ran out of the kitchen, desperate to avoid a fight, and turned left as Hurm had instructed. At the end of the hallway was the staircase and the way was clear. Gresten sprinted as fast as he could and dashed down the stairs.

As the prince emerged into the next corridor, he could see two wardens approaching him. They were grinning as though they were enjoying this. Gresten ran forward and raised his hands. He emitted a shockwave that knocked both of the demons to the floor with two heavy thuds. Seizing his chance, he ran forward and jumped over them, barely managing to escape their dazed grasps.

There it was; the window lay ahead. Gresten did not feel good about this leap of faith, but he climbed onto the windowsill. He dropped the sack containing his armour into the water below. With a final look over his shoulder, he took a deep breath and dove forward, falling fifty feet into the river below.

The prince hit the water and fell beneath the surface. The flow of the river was strong. and he could feel himself moving downriver immediately. He could see the sack of armour sinking and he swam forward to it. It wasn't light, but Gresten was strong enough to pull it with him.

Gresten kicked furiously and tried to pull himself forward with one arm toward the eastern riverbank. It was exhausting and took all of his strength, but he eventually reached the muddy bank. He walked towards the treeline, threw his armour on the ground, and fell down laughing. He did it. He was free.

It took almost ten minutes for Hurm to arrive, but he showed up as he said he would. Gresten wasn't sure what to make of his mysterious masked saviour, but he was certainly grateful.

"I must say, Prince Gresten," uttered Hurm, "I wasn't sure that you would make it when I first climbed up to your cell."

"How did you climb so high?" asked Gresten.

"Years of practising. I've lived in this my whole life. I've seen it at highs, and I've seen it at lows, but it became clear a decade ago that the lowest lows would come soon. I had to be ready for anything."

"Will you tell me who you are?"

"Who I am is not important. I have my reasons for never showing my face. Do not take it to heart, I don't show it to anybody."

Gresten expected an answer somewhat like this.

"What now?" asked the prince.

"We have a few hours until sunrise. I was able to find you spare garments, a sword, and a knife. That's why I'm late, so I apologise for that. Put these on and I'll start a fire before you freeze to death."

"Thank you, Hurm," said Gresten sincerely as Hurm tossed the clothes to Gresten and dropped the sword at his feet.

"Are you hungry?" asked Hurm. "I hope you don't mind rat because that's all we've got to eat."

"Rat will do. Are we safe to wait here?"

"Yes, I expect so."

Hurm gathered sticks and began to light a fire while Gresten put on his new garments and his armour. The prince's armour felt a little looser than it had before his incarceration. No matter, he would eat a feast when he next had the opportunity.

Gresten and Hurm sat by the fire as Hurm cooked a couple of rats.

"Hurm, how did you know that I would be executed?" asked Gresten.

Hurm let out a low chuckle. "I lied about that."

Gresten was shocked. "I wasn't going to be executed?"

"Not to my knowledge, no."

"Then why did you tell me I was?"

"To force you to action. I was doing you a favour by making you set yourself free. You're better off away from this city, Gresten. We don't need more members of the royal family dying here."

"A good knight died because I rushed my escape."

"As was his duty. What do you think knights are for?"

"This was not the way."

"It worked, did it not? You are here."

Gresten sat in silence, unsure what to say next. It was true that he was free, yes, but Sir Brand's life meant something. Gresten thought about what he said to Sir Brand, about how he returned to save Altburg. It was as much of a lie as what Hurm had told Gresten.

"What must be done to save this city?" asked the prince.

"Save it? There's no saving it," replied Hurm incredulously.

"Humour me. Let's say there was the smallest of chances."

Hurm did not answer right away. "Well, you would want to kill Za'gerath's generals. Killing them would weaken his influence. They were once servants of King Gerath before turning into demons."

"Where can I find them? How can I kill them?"

"There are four nearby. There is the Foreman, the Tentacular Horror, and the Fair Lady. The

Bridge Guardian, who you've already met, is the fourth. He was once a man named Guardian Volek. Did you know that? He prided himself on keeping the city free of criminality, but as the city fell, he made his own deal with a demon and became what he is today."

"Where can I find the other three?"

"The Foreman is in the Caves of Cavaurus, where the gold was once mined in the kingdom. The Tentacular Horror is in Asmuth Swamp much further down the river."

"What about the Fair Lady that you mentioned?"

Hurm hesitated. "Are you truly planning to kill all of these demons?"

"I had not considered anything like this until an hour ago, but now I think that I must. I lied to Sir Brand that I would do it and he gave his life for me. I cannot live without trying to keep my word."

"Fine," sighed Hurm, "you can leave the Fair Lady and the Bridge Guardian to me. They are both within the main city. I'm more skilled than you at traversing this place and, frankly, not getting thrown into a cell."

"Thank you, Hurm," said Gresten.

"You're welcome, Prince. I must take my leave now, but to reach the caves you must follow the riverbank westward for a mile. It serves as a tunnel in and out of the city walls. If you deal with the Foreman in the caves, then you can reach the swamp by passing through one of the exits there. Again, just follow the river."

Hurm climbed to his feet to leave, but Gresten had another question for him.

"Why are you helping me?"

"I promised your mother that I would keep you alive should you ever come back to Altburg."

"My mother?"

Hurm didn't respond and walked off into the night, leaving Gresten alone to ponder what he had said.

Chapter 5

Hunting in the Deep

Gresten, alone again, walked downriver on the bank of the Runder in the morning sun. He didn't have his map anymore, but he had a rough idea of where he was. Altburg was a big city, home to more than just houses and towers. The small forest here was once used as a private hunting ground by the dukes, barons, and various other nobles. It was the perfect spot to break away from civilisation without truly leaving the comforts of the city.

It was a peaceful morning, with no demons to speak of and only the rushing river to listen to. It was the first time Gresten truly felt at peace since his brief stay with Saint Rudolph. He enjoyed the short stroll even with the knowledge he had a difficult journey ahead.

As he rounded a bend, Gresten could see the entrance to the Caves of Cavaurus ahead. It was a large archway built into the cliffside, supported by stone pillars and wooden beams. A few old carts and barrels littered the area outside. Hung on a hook nearby was a lantern. Gresten checked to see if there was still oil left and was dismayed to see that it was empty.

"You won't get very far with that empty lantern," came a voice from inside the cave entrance.

"Who goes there?" said Gresten, drawing his sword.

"Don't get all jumpy, lad. I mean no harm," said the voice as a figure emerged from the shadows.

The man standing before Gresten was a burly fellow who looked to be in his early thirties. He had dark scruffy hair and a scratchy beard. The man didn't look particularly imposing.

"My name is Gresten. Please tell me yours," said Gresten with his hand still on the handle of his sword.

"Alright, son," said the man. "You need to learn to be a bit more trusting when you find fellow living folks in this wretched city. My name is Horban of Roch, but you can just call me Horban."

"Well met, Horban," said Gresten as he released his grip on his sword. He remained alert but didn't want to give Horban reason to mistrust him.

"Well met yourself, Gresten," said Horban.

"Were you waiting for somebody? Why were you lurking in this entrance?"

"Nah, lad. I was taking a rest. Filled with demons this here cave, you see. Most of them are slogging away mining for gold and won't bother you, but the slave drivers? They're a little trickier."

"You've been inside already?"

"Yeah, a few times. I'm a treasure hunter, you see. Got to bring in the gold somehow and where better than a literal gold mine, eh?"

"Did you happen across the Foreman inside?"

"If I see any sign of him approaching, I make a run for the door. He's no whelp, that's for sure."

Gresten paused for a moment before responding. "Horban, I have a proposal for you. If you can guide me through here with your light, I'll help you tackle these slave drivers you speak of. I ask for no stake in the spoils, any gold found is yours to keep."

Horban's eyes narrowed slightly. "Guide you through? To where exactly?"

"To the Foreman."

"What's your plan here, Gresten?"

"I'm something of a demon hunter. Once I kill the Foreman and help you with these slave drivers, it'll be an easy place for you to hunt for your treasure. It's a mutually beneficial proposal."

"Say no more, I'm in," said Horban. He approached Gresten and offered his hand to shake. Gresten shook it and gave Horban a nod of thanks.

"Do you have a lantern?" asked Gresten.

"I have better," said Horban.

Gresten watched as Horban put his hands together and focused. He drew them apart slowly and, as he did so, a small orb of light appeared. It began to hover around Horban.

"A little something a priest friend of mine taught me," said Horban with a chuckle.

"Perhaps you can teach me that spell after we're done in here," said Gresten.

"If this goes well, I'd be happy to."

Horban led the way down the tunnel. Gresten

had to walk carefully because of the minecart tracks embedded in the brown stone. He had to admit that having a free hand while Horban lit the way was preferable to holding a lantern.

The duo walked for several minutes down the mostly straight path before Horban steered them to a small room built into the tunnel walls. Inside was a chair and small desk, long empty, and a wooden staircase at the back.

"Everything at the surface has been picked clean. We've got to go deep to find both gold and your quarry, lad."

Horban led Gresten down the staircase that led to another room, similar to the first. They walked out into the tunnel and followed the straight path ahead.

The air was thick and damp. Gresten could tell that he wouldn't want to exert himself too much before facing the Foreman. It was not a good environment for a drawn-out battle. Quick and clean, that would be the way.

"Here again, Horban?" enquired a squeaky voice from the ground.

"Alvaro? What are you doing here?" demanded Horban.

Alvaro stood up from where he was lying on the ground. He was a scrawny-looking man with a shaved head and rat-like face. He was wearing leather armour while holding a short sword in one hand and a dagger in the other. Strapped to his back was a small crossbow.

"Same thing you're doing, mate," said Alvaro. "Who's your friend?"

"It's of no concern of yours, worm," said Horban defiantly.

"There's no need to be so rude," Alvaro said with a smirk. "We're all friends in Altburg, right? We got to stick together against the demons."

"Last warning, Alvaro. Get out of here before I kill you."

Alvaro laughed and ran off in the direction that Gresten and Horban had come from.

"Is there bad blood there?" asked Gresten.

"There's a reason they call that man Alvaro the Worm," said Horban with a stern face. "He's another one, like myself, that tries to find treasure in Altburg. I would call myself a treasure hunter because I only take what is no longer being used. Alvaro is a thief. He takes from the living and dead alike. He has a tendency to ensure that the living are dead so their treasure is his to keep, if you catch my drift."

"Should I still heed your advice about being more trusting of other living individuals in the city?"

"You've got me there, lad. Alvaro is most certainly one of the exceptions."

"Then why let him live?" asked Gresten.

"I ask myself that every time I come across him. I suppose it's in the hope that even a rotten thief like him can redeem himself eventually. Naïve of me, perhaps, but it's the way I am."

After a few more minutes of walking down the tunnel, Gresten spotted a light coming from ahead. The tunnel opened up into a small cavern with a pool of water covering most of the ground beneath. A stone bridge connected the tunnel to the far side of the room, but a staircase near the halfway point led to the ground below that bordered on the water. Gresten could see a small firepit nestled in the rocky terrain.

"The coast is clear for now," whispered Horban, as his orb of light dimmed then faded away. "We'll creep along and wait for one of the guards to come back, lad. We've had an easy ride so far, but not for much longer."

The pair walked to the staircase, keeping an eye on the ground below. Horban led Gresten down the staircase, past the firepit, and over to the entrance of another tunnel. Amidst the crackling of the fire, Gresten could hear the occasional raspy yell coming from deeper in the caves, as well as the sound of metal hitting stone.

Horban leaned over to peer around the corner into the tunnel. "Nothing coming for now. We'll wait a couple of minutes to see if anybody comes back this way. Slave drivers are easy to spot. Tall fellas with ash-grey skin, two long horns, and red-trimmed armour. Trick is to go for the head."

It took less than a minute for Gresten's ears to perk up again. He could hear the clinking and shuffling of metal armour coming closer. He held his hand up to Horban and gestured for him to step back. Horban did so.

As the demon walked past them towards the firepit, Gresten swung his sword horizontally through the air and cleaved the slave driver's head clean off. Its body fell to the ground and the head followed shortly after.

Horban checked around the corner to make sure the tunnel was empty. "Easy as that, lad. Stealth is definitely our friend down here, but we'll need to be ready for a real fight eventually."

"Yes, but let's take the opportunities when they present themselves," said Gresten, who dragged the slave driver's body into the pool of water. He grabbed the demon's head by one of the horns and threw it in too.

"No arguments from me," said Horban.

The duo crept through the tunnel, which eventually opened up into a larger cavern. Everything here was well lit by torches and lanterns scattered throughout. Gresten looked around and could see the miners at work. They looked similar to the whelps from the city above, but they were dressed in even worse rags and had a horrible, swollen hump on their back. They were continually hunched over with their pickaxes, even when drawing them overhead to swing.

"Watch this," said Horban with a sly smile. He walked over to one of the miners and waved his hand in front of its face. The demon did not react and merely continued to swing its pickaxe.

"They're very focused on their task," said Gresten.

"Obsessed, I'd say. They won't bother you unless you stop them mining."

Gresten and Horban walked further into the cavern and could see two slave drivers patrolling up ahead. They didn't seem to need to patrol considering the obsessive work ethic of the miners, but Gresten wondered if the miners mined so hard because of the threat of the slave drivers punishing them. If his theory was true and the miners were humans, perhaps he would have felt pity.

Horban grabbed a rock the tossed it at the slave drivers, before ducking behind a stalagmite. The two slave drivers yelled at each other in a demonic tongue before one approached to investigate. Gresten leapt out to fight it as Horban tried to pull him back.

Gresten's sword collided with the slave driver's own sword. Gresten kicked his opponent back before thrusting his blade at its head. The demon rolled backwards and Gresten only just had enough time to duck as a fireball narrowly missed his head.

"I forgot to warn you about their magic," lamented Horban as he ran towards the second slave driver who had thrown the fireball.

The slave driver Gresten was fighting was back on his feet and swung his sword vertically down at Gresten, who parried with his own sword. Gresten forced his enemy's sword aside and swung again at its head, this time cutting off one of its horns. The demon yelled with rage in its horrific language and two miners ran to its defence.

The prince made quick work of one of the clumsy miners with a swift hack at its neck. The other miner raised its pickaxe overhead and brought it down at Gresten, but he leapt back in time. The slave driver he had been fighting threw a fireball his way, but Gresten instinctively raised his sword at it. The fireball collided with it and fizzled out.

The slave driver and remaining miner charged as Gresten raised his hand and used his Push spell, knocking both of his enemies to the ground. He ran to the slave driver and pierced its head with his sword before it had a chance to react. He cleaved the head from the miner as it tried to lumber back to its feet.

Gresten ran over to Horban who had just finished dealing with the other slave driver. Both men were no worse for the wear, all things considered.

"How did you forget about the fireballs?" asked Gresten, panting.

"I'm incredibly sorry, lad," said Horban earnestly.

"It's fine, all is well. We handled them. Do you want to take any of the ore from this room or save your treasure for the way back?"

"No, my friend. There are plenty of coins and bars being pressed below. The city may have stopped, but the work did not. The real riches are further in, and the ore is too heavy to carry."

Horban passed his flask of water to Gresten who took a swig. The prince thanked him and Horban led Gresten into one of the tunnels connected to this cavern.

"Are we close?" asked Gresten a few rooms and many slave drivers later.

"The Foreman is never in a fixed spot, so I'm getting you as close as my best guess allows," admitted Horban.

"That's alright, Horban. I could have wandered this place for days had I entered alone. I'm thankful for all of your help so far."

"I'm thankful for yours too, lad. I usually take the quieter approach and would be a couple of hours behind trying to find the right timing to take the demons one-on-one."

The two continued through the hot tunnels and caverns, across bridges, and down staircases. It was stifling, but the men pushed on. The Foreman was nowhere to be seen, but they came across treasure aplenty. Horban's eyes lit up at the sight of the gold, but he resisted the temptation to lift any until the return journey.

Gresten made good use of his swordsmanship to deal with the demons while holding back his magic unless he was in a tight spot. True to what Saint Rudolph had said, Gresten could feel his divine energy weakening with each passing use.

"Stop," said Horban as they walked down a stone staircase. He gestured towards a narrow window in the wall beside him and moved aside for Gresten to look through.

Gresten could see into a cavern where there were more miners, but also a much larger figure. That must be him. The Foreman. Even with his hunched frame, he stood about ten feet tall. He had two horns on his head which splintered into three more halfway up. He dragged a large war hammer behind him that glowed a faint red and across his torso was tightly strapped plate armour that looked uncomfortably positioned.

"He's smaller than the Bridge Guardian," whispered Gresten, "but I am still wary."

"I will aid you in the fight, Gresten," said Horban. "A mutually beneficial arrangement, like you said."

"Thank you, Horban. You're a good man."

"Think nothing of it, lad. I haven't been this deep before but knowing how this place is built…I think there must be a tunnel underneath us somewhere."

The two men walked down the staircase hoping to avoid any more attention from slave drivers that may be patrolling nearby. Horban's guess was correct, there was a small series of tunnels beneath the staircase that eventually led to the entrance of the cavern where the Foreman wandered. He appeared to be circling the room as though keeping an eye on the miners. Gresten was relieved to see that it was only him and the miners, however, he was concerned about the number of miners this time.

"There are plenty of rocks in the cavern to hide behind," said Gresten. "I think we should use the cover they provide to take out the miners. He can probably call them to his aid like the slave drivers could."

"I agree, lad," replied Horban. "He's patrolling clockwise so we'll wait for him to reach the furthest side of the room, near that tunnel over there, and then go clockwise ourselves to keep our distance."

"He may realise what's happening once he sees the dead miners. In that case, I'll keep him occupied while you dispatch the other miners."

Horban nodded. "Yes, lad. I'll see it done."

Gresten and Horban waited for the Foreman to reach the furthest point at the far side of the cavern and the pair then slipped into the room unnoticed. They made quick work of the mining miners and sought cover between kills. Gresten beheaded them while Horban grabbed their pickaxes to stop them from clunking on the ground. The duo picked up the pace to gain slightly on the Foreman, hoping to avoid him noticing their handiwork too soon.

The Foreman suddenly roared an unholy roar. He swung around and threw his hammer over his shoulder. He had noticed the dead miners and surveyed the room enraged. He couldn't see who or what had committed such an atrocity, but he knew that something was attacking his crew and he would not stand for it.

Gresten and Horban remained low behind a

boulder as the Foreman charged around the room examining the bodies of his workers. The two men knew this was their last chance to clear out the miners. They nodded to each other and ran into the open to attack the miners that remained. It wasn't long before the Foreman spun around once again and saw the two invaders, both mid-swing.

"There are only six remaining, lad," yelled Horban.

Gresten ran towards the centre of the room and taunted the Foreman. "Over here, you lummox. I am your target!"

The Foreman charged at Gresten with his war hammer held high above his head. Gresten waited until the running monster swung and then dove forward between the Foreman's legs. As he did so, he slashed upwards in an arc with his sword cutting a deep gash into the Foreman's right thigh. The slick slice of the prince's blade almost seemed to echo for a second before the Foreman yelled in pain and drowned it out. The master of the mines thrashed his feet wildly, kicking Gresten to the ground and knocking the prince's sword from his hands.

Suddenly, a heavy pickaxe swung through the air and the prince's eyes widened in horror. He raised his hands to block the attack but felt a prayer flow through him. His Push spell diverted the miner demon's pickaxe and it wedged itself into the dirt as its owner tried to pull it out.

The prince climbed to his feet as the Foreman charged towards him. He hurried around the miner who was still desperately trying to free his tool, only for the Foreman to flatten his own worker.

Gresten grabbed hold of the pickaxe and pulled it free. Spinning around, Gresten unleashed his new weapon. It hurled around as it flew towards the Foreman before tearing a chunk from the fearsome demon's neck. As the demon howled in pain once more, it slammed its fist into the prince's chest, taking him back down to the ground.

The prince climbed to his feet and narrowly evaded a kick from the Foreman. The profusely bleeding demon leaned forward and charged at Gresten, knocking him to the ground and pinning him down. Gresten tried to use his Push spell to escape the grapple, but the hulking demon had restricted his wrists and he could not find the right angle. As Gresten struggled, he could feel the intensity of the heat radiating from the Foreman's hammer and the demon raised it, ready to crush the prince underneath its infernal weapon.

Horban killed the last of the miners and bolted to Gresten's aid, unwilling to let his new friend meet a terrible fate. The Foreman turned and swung his hammer at Horban, knocking the Rochian into the air and burning a hole through his armour.

Gresten pulled a hand free and jammed his fingers into the Foreman's bleeding neck. It winced and shifted its weight, giving the prince a brief moment to escape. He ran to his sword, picked it up and slashed at the Foreman's heel as the beast stood, bringing the demon back down and onto his knees.

Gresten leapt onto his back, wrapping one arm around his neck and raising his sword high. The demon struggled and tried to shake off the prince, swinging its hammer wildly, but only hitting and melting its own armour. With a powerful thrust of his sword, the prince impaled the Foreman through the neck. The demon collapsed to the ground, dead, joining his miners.

Not taking a second to rest, Gresten climbed off the beast and ran to help Horban to his feet. "Are you alright, Horban?"

"Never...better, lad," wheezed Horban. "He wasn't so tough in the end."

"I don't believe this would have gone half as well had you not been here," Gresten admitted.

"Good thing that I wa—"

Horban's response was stopped abruptly as a bolt pierced the side of his skull and he fell to the floor, joining the Foreman and the miners in death.

Chapter 6

Disrespecting the Dead

Gresten turned and used his Push spell to deflect a bolt heading straight for him before diving behind one of the boulders nearby. Somebody was targeting them from the window they first spied the Foreman from.

"I thank ye for clearing out the worst of the beasties down here," came the squeaky voice of Alvaro the Worm. He followed up with a slight chuckle.

Gresten stayed silent. The shock of losing his new friend Horban after such a valiant victory left him speechless.

"You can't stay back there forever, friend," called Alvaro. "I never did catch your name. That Horban never really introduced us now, did he? Care to enlighten me?"

Gresten remained silent. If he was able to

escape to the staircase, Alvaro could still lie in wait for him. This smaller, arguably less demonic foe made him even more uneasy than the Foreman did. He couldn't rely on being able to use his sword and magic to deflect the bolts for long.

The prince realised that his only certain way of escape was to run for the other tunnel at the far side of the room. He grabbed a chunk of ore from the ground and hurled it over the boulder and, sure enough, a bolt struck it.

Gresten ran hard while using a steady barrage of his spells to repel any bolts that may strike him. It took less than ten seconds to reach the tunnel, but it felt a lot longer. The prince hurled himself around the corner to make sure he was in cover.

This cavern was free from further demons and several rays of light trickled in from the far side of the cavern wall. Gresten breathed a short sigh of relief and ran to the far side to see if he could find a way out.

There it was. A final short tunnel that led to freedom from this hot and humid series of stone rooms. Gresten glanced behind him to make sure that Alvaro wasn't following and ran through the tunnel and towards the open air.

An ocean of fields expanded before him. Dotted throughout the landscape were a few small houses that would have once been farms but would certainly be abandoned considering the state of affairs in Altburg.

Gresten had a rough idea of where he was. He had entered the caves and emerged beyond the western wall of the city. He knew a small, wooded area lay to the south and if he could cross the Runder River further to the west and head north, he would reach Asmuth Swamp. Hurm had told him that's where the Tentacular Horror awaited him.

The prince followed the river for a while trying to put as much distance between himself and the Caves of Cavaurus as he could. He wanted to make sure that Alvaro couldn't attack him from a distance. Once he was satisfied with this, he knelt down and made a prayer to The True One asking for Horban of Roch's soul to reach the Inner World.

As Prince Gresten continued to walk down the river, he wondered if he should follow the city walls south to find his horse, Hilda. He hoped that she was enjoying her longer-than-intended stay in the field he left her in. At least she wasn't likely to be disturbed there.

Gresten could see a bridge up ahead with what looked to be a small, abandoned inn beside it. As he approached, the prince spotted a wooden signpost swaying lightly in the cool, evening breeze.

"The Runderside Inn. Rest your weary head and drown your sorrows away," read Gresten quietly.

"Rest your weary head after almost drowning is a more accurate sign these days," came a voice.

Gresten looked around to see who had spoken to him. The voice was familiar and the owner of it slowly emerged. He was in a full set of dark armour and his face was obscured by his helmet grill.

"Master Reinhold?" asked Gresten, shocked to see him alive and well.

"In the flesh inside the metal," chortled Reinhold. "It is good to see you alive, Master Gresten."

"You're alright? I thought that surely you had died in the river weeks ago."

"I thought that surely you had been crushed by the Bridge Guardian weeks ago," said Reinhold.

"I am thankful that we're both more fortunate than the other presumed," said Gresten.

"Indeed," said Reinhold as he gestured inside. "Come rest up here and tell me of your tale since we last met. I assure you it's safe in this inn."

Reinhold led Gresten inside the run-down, but surprisingly cosy, inn. The room was lit by the orange light shining through the dusty windows. Reinhold had clearly been using the tables and chairs as barriers to ward off any invaders in the night. He righted one of the tables and two of the chairs.

"Shall I start?" asked Reinhold as he sat on a chair. "I suspect my story is shorter than yours."

"Feel free, my friend," said Gresten as he sat on the chair opposite.

"I fell in the river, I could barely keep myself afloat after the Bridge Guardian broke my arm, I woke up on a bank halfway to Asmuth Swamp, I wandered here and began nursing myself back to health. That sums it up nicely, I would say."

"Your arm is healed already? It hasn't even been a month yet."

Reinhold laughed. "There are many more ways to heal yourself than simply using natural methods. I am a man of many skills. Sadly, fighting giant demons of stone is not one of them. Now tell me of your tale, my friend."

"I was able to slip past the Bridge Guardian and found a pair of wardens waiting for me at the far side. I was thrown into the cells for weeks, but I was able to escape with the help of a stranger named Hurm and a fellow prisoner. Sadly, the other prisoner did not make it out."

"I'm sorry to hear that," lamented Reinhold.

"His name was Sir Brand. He was a good man. After I escaped, Hurm and I parted ways and I passed through the Caves of Cavaurus. A treasure hunter named Horban of Roch aided me and we killed the Foreman before he was murdered by a thief. That was barely a couple of hours ago."

"It seems as though a lot of people who team up with you meet an unfortunate end," scoffed Reinhold before catching himself on. "Forgive me, that was unnecessary. You say you killed the Foreman?"

Gresten was irked by Reinhold's comment but decided to let it go. "Yes. He's dead, along with many of his slave drivers and miners. Do you know anything of him?"

Reinhold paused. "Yes, I know of him. In fact, I knew him back when he was a human. He was once a revered knight called Sir Paudorf of Lochmeria. He was most famous for slaying the leviathan of Lake Roh. A once-loyal advisor to King Gerath who turned foul not long after the emergence of Za'gerath."

"How did he become the Foreman?" asked Gresten, eager to know more.

"That, I do not know. I would suspect he made a deal with a demon. Perhaps his will was broken, and he left himself vulnerable to losing his body and mind. It can happen in many ways, but those are the two most common."

Gresten contemplated this for a moment before steering the conversation elsewhere. "If you're planning to return to Altburg, then the caves would be one of the safest ways to get into the heart of the city. Is that your intent?"

"It is. I've got business to attend to in the castle. I'll find another way to deal with the Bridge Guardian, but it's useful to know there may be wardens waiting on the other side. Thank you for the information, sire."

"Sire?"

"Pardon me, I meant to say sir," said Reinhold.

Gresten knew it was not a mispronunciation. Reinhold knew exactly who Gresten was. The prince wondered why he would fake a slip of the tongue. Gresten pondered whether or not Reinhold had known since they first met, or if something more had happened in the last couple of weeks that he had not told Gresten about.

"What next for you, Master Gresten?" asked Reinhold, breaking the silence.

"I'm going to the graveyard to kill the Tentacular Horror."

"In Asmuth Swamp? Seeking glory, are you?"

Reinhold's attitude was starting to grate on Gresten. "No. Hurm told me that if his strongest allies are killed, Za'gerath will weaken. That will make it easier to find my brother's heirloom in the castle."

"Is that true?" asked Reinhold.

"I've wondered that myself, but fewer demons left to plague our world is a good thing regardless."

"That's fair. You'll want to seek out Lady Silke then. I doubt you'll be much of a match for the Horror if you're going to fight it alone in its domain."

"Who is Lady Silke?"

"The Witch of Asmuth. If you know much of these lands, maybe that'll sound more familiar."

"Sadly, I know nothing of her. How would she help me?"

"She's a powerful witch that's known to teach magic to those who seek her out. She knows a little of everything from chaos magic to divine magic and even infernal magic used by the demons themselves."

"Do you know where I can find her in the swamp?"

"If she wants you to find her, she'll show you the way," said Reinhold as he arose. "Now, I must take my leave if I want to enter the caves. I don't know how long it will be before the death of the Foreman is noticed and the place is swarming with more demons."

Gresten stood up to see Reinhold to the door.

"Take care of yourself, Master Reinhold," said Gresten.

"You too, Master Gresten."

Gresten watched Reinhold depart and made sure that he was really gone. Something was not right and Gresten couldn't put his finger on what, but he didn't want to risk staying here. Perhaps Reinhold would take care of Alvaro and make things easier for Gresten in the future. The prince walked off into the plains to find another abandoned building where he hoped he could find scraps of food and shelter for the night.

*

The stench of the swamp filled Gresten's nostrils as he hopped across the soggy ground to reach the drier parts. It was stomach-turning when he first entered the swamp and it was little better now. He was certainly very grateful that his leather boots weren't letting in the filth water and his feet remained clean otherwise they would have stunk for weeks.

Gresten watched as a hand emerged from the water in front of him. The hand was pale and swollen, but it had enough strength to dig its nails deep into the ground and pull the rest of its body out from the swamp waters. The bloated and decaying corpse lunged at Gresten, hoping he would join it in its deep grave, but Gresten plunged his sword into its skull before kicking it back into the water.

Gresten wiped his sword on the grass and continued deeper into the swamp. That was not the first corpse that had made an attempt on his life today and it would certainly not be the last. He had been wandering for hours in search of any sign of Lady Silke or the Tentacular Horror, but he had no luck so far. Considering the swamp was almost the size of Altburg itself this was no surprise. He would keep going until he found something, anything, but he was keenly aware that he would have to sleep eventually.

Another corpse dragged itself from the depths, but Gresten thought it better to save his energy. These undead were slow and, even with the swampy terrain, he was agile enough to outpace them. He had to play it smart here, lest he join them in the water before too long. He moved further along and eventually reached a wet, but stable, path.

"A guide would be very useful," Gresten uttered under his breath.

Within seconds, a small floating orb appeared before him. Unlike the one Horban had summoned in the caves, this orb was a deep red as though made from ethereal fragments of rubies. Gresten wasn't sure what to make of the orb. Magic coming seemingly out of nowhere was never a good sign, but perhaps this was what Reinhold had meant about the witch wanting to be found.

"Did Lady Silke send you?" asked Gresten.

The orb merely hovered slowly up and down, not reacting to his words. Gresten wondered whether this was a creature or merely an extension of the witch's powers. Perhaps it was both...perhaps it was neither.

"Show me the way and I will follow," he said. It was reckless, Gresten knew that, but he wasn't sure that he would even be able to find his way out now that he was this deep in the swamp. It would be impossible to retrace his steps having come so far and with so many undead having crawled over his footprints.

The orb began to move forwards along the path and Gresten followed. He was uneasy, but he had decided to deal with any problems as they reared their heads.

Gresten continued to follow the orb for nearly an hour, occasionally stopping to deal with a persistent corpse that emerged from the waters; the less persistent ones were ignored. The orb began to guide Gresten into the waters, and he hesitated.

"I will not follow you into the water," Gresten

told the orb defiantly, remaining upon the mucky ground. He knew he was being reckless in following it, but this was a step too far.

The orb moved back from the waters and towards Gresten. It flashed a brighter red a couple of times, and a pathway of raised stones erupted from the pool, sending faint ripples out. The orb then proceeded over this new path.

Gresten walked forward after the orb. As he reached the halfway point of the sequence of stones, they faded into nothing and Gresten plummeted into the water below. He had to wrench his arms from the mud to stand up, but his feet were trapped. The corpses began to stir and move beneath the water towards him, barely visible in the dim light.

Gresten grabbed his sword and stabbed wildly at the disturbed water, but the undead were coming faster than he could kill them and their murky liquid shield made it all the more difficult to see where they were.

The orb floated towards Gresten, and a voice echoed from within. "Beg for my help."

"Who are you?" yelled Gresten as he thrust furiously.

"I want you to beg for my help," the orb stated calmly. The voice sounded feminine but powerful.

"I will not beg!" Gresten shouted as he slashed at the orb, unable to reach it.

"Are you sure?" asked the orb.

"I will see the Inner World before I beg for my life, Lady Silke," stated Gresten as he felt the hands of the corpses wrap around his legs and slowly start to pull him under.

"Good," said the orb. "Perhaps you can be

taught something that requires iron will."

The orb faded from sight and Gresten felt his body sink further into the water, dragged down by the swollen fingers of the bloated corpses trying to make him one of their own. His final thought as his head was pulled beneath the water was of his unkept promise to Sir Brand. He had tried, even if it were all for nought.

Chapter 7

The Priestess and the Knight

Gresten awoke on a warm wooden floor, wearing only his undergarments. He was dry and he was alive. He wanted to sit up, but he was tired. He was more tired than he had ever been in his life. He waited for another moment before forcing himself into a seated position.

Surveying his surroundings, he appeared to be in a small cabin. There was still a little daylight outside, and he could see the trees of the swamp. The cabin was modestly furnished, and many plants and herbs adorned the walls and various surfaces. A lit fireplace heated the room and there was a beautiful woman sitting on a small chair beside it watching Gresten.

"You're awake, my dear," said the woman softly. Her voice was the voice from the orb. She had a youthful face, no older than eighteen, with long pure-white hair going past her shoulders. She wore a purple dress with a red ribbon tied around her waist. Draped over her shoulders was a black cloak.

"Are you Lady Silke?" asked Gresten.

"Yes, young prince," she replied with a smile.

"You know who I am?"

"You're the spitting image of your brother, Germund. Oh my, I haven't seen him in quite some time. When I was last in the city a few years ago, in fact. Is he well?"

"I have not seen him in quite some time either, Lady Silke."

Lady Silke cocked her head to the side. "Are you sure?"

"Quite sure," said Gresten. He looked around, trying to find something to cover himself with. "Where are my clothes?"

"I hung them outside to dry, Prince. Let me bring them inside."

Lady Silke arose as though it was no effort to stand and appeared to glide out her door, which slowly opened as she approached. Moments later, she returned holding Gresten's clothes. She turned to face the fireplace as he put them on.

"Were you testing me with the orb?" asked Gresten.

"Yes," Lady Silke replied simply.

"For what purpose?"

"You're here to rid Lochmeria of the demons, no? I needed to see how compliant you were and how strong your will was. There may have been simpler ways, but I always have fun using my orbs."

"I passed?"

"Yes. You let me guide you, but you also refused to beg when I asked for something unreasonable. That was enough to satisfy me."

Lady Silke walked over to her table and poured a fragrant tea that she passed to Gresten. Gresten drank a mouthful without thinking and burned his tongue.

"Silly boy," said Lady Silke. She waved her hands and a rush of cool air shot at the cup. It did not spill the tea, but Gresten could see the steam had stopped rising.

Gresten took a sip before speaking again. "I was told to seek you out by a man named Reinhold."

"I do not know a Reinhold," said Lady Silke nonchalantly. "Perhaps he knows of me, rather than knowing me personally. Are you certain his name was Reinhold?"

"I'm certain it was Reinhold."

"You're certain he told you it was Reinhold. Is that correct?"

She was right, but Gresten was a little irritated by her mannerisms. "Yes," he grunted.

"If you're looking for training in magic, I can help you. I will spare you three months of my time, but that is all I can afford to spare. I welcome your attempt to rid Lochmeria of the demons, but I have other important work that cannot be put on hold beyond that. I will teach you four spells. Are you familiar with the schools?"

Gresten nodded. "I am. Chaos magic used by the

mages, divine magic used by the clerics and infernal magic used by the sorcerers."

"Excellent. I can tell that you already possess an inkling of divine magical skill, but it is simply a trifle. I will teach you two chaos spells and two divine spells. You will have mastered them before you leave, but you are never to attempt an infernal spell. No matter what you read, no matter what you think. You are not to play with this corrupting force. Do you understand?"

"I understand," said Gresten affirmatively.

"Then we shall begin right away," said Lady Silke with a sly smile.

*

"I told you to concentrate on the corpse. I will let it kill you if it reaches you," warned Lady Silke.

Gresten didn't reply. He tried to channel his anger into casting his Fireball spell. Divine magic used a clear-minded focus with a willed prayer, whereas chaos magic used unleashed emotion. It was difficult to go back and forth between the two, but Lady Silke had been training Gresten for the past week at rotating his spells.

It had taken him two months to master using each of the spells she had taught him. The first was the divine Orb of Light, a spell he had hoped to learn from Horban. The second divine spell was Healing Hands, which allowed him to heal minor wounds. The first chaos spell was Heat, a spell that let Gresten channel intense heat through his weapon. He now realised that the Foreman had used this on his war hammer. The second chaos spell was a favourite of the slave drivers, Fireball.

Gresten focused on the thought of Alvaro the Worm killing Horban and he forced a fireball from the palm of his hand.

"Good, now knock him back," ordered Lady Silke.

Gresten tried to rid his mind of any thoughts and emitted a Push from the same hand. It had worked! The corpse fell backwards and dissipated into nothing.

"That was the quickest yet," said Lady Silke sounding pleased. "The corpses in the rest of the swamp, however, will not be my illusions. You can count on the Tentacular Horror to not be one too."

"I know," said Gresten. "I still have not forgiven you for convincing me I was going to die when you were testing me."

Lady Silke laughed. "I am not a sadist, as you should know by now. I am merely a trickster when I need to make a point."

Gresten laughed too. He wasn't truly angry. He had come to accept that Lady Silke was kind and wise, even if from a distance she seemed downright terrifying.

"When you have lived as many centuries as I, you must find new ways to amuse yourself while getting your work done."

"Centuries?" asked Gresten. Lady Silke had always been rather sensitive about her age.

Lady Silke paused, realising what she had said.

"Oh bother," she sighed.

"I won't tell a soul, Lady Silke. I presume you would see to it that I was dead if I did."

Lady Silke relented. "I'm three-hundred and seventy-seven years old. Over a century of that spent in this swamp."

"You still look younger than I do," said the twenty-two-year-old prince with a chuckle.

"The power of alchemy and illusion," said Lady Silke with a sly smile.

For a split second, Gresten was certain that he could see a flash of wrinkles appear on her skin and Lady Silke's eyes sink deeper into her face. He blinked hard and looked again, but her face was its usual youthful self.

*

"Push. Fireball. Orb. Heat. Strike the corpse. Push again. Fireball," ordered Lady Silke in rapid succession.

Gresten obeyed each step until she dissipated the illusory bloated corpse. His training was complete today.

"Perfect, my dear," said Lady Silke as the corpse faded into nothing. "I have a parting gift for you if you would wait by the stairs.

Lady Silke drifted forwards and up into the cabin. She returned moments later, holding a beautifully crafted longsword. Its guard and pommel bore a golden sheen with a large red ruby inserted in the pommel and three smaller rubies encrusted in the guard.

"For you, young prince," said Lady Silke, passing the blade to Gresten.

"I thank you for such a wonderful gift, my Lady," said Gresten. He kneeled as he took the blade. "I thank you for the time and effort you have given me over the last three months. I have learned so much and I will endeavour to rid Altburg of Za'gerath."

"You are welcome, young apprentice," replied the witch with a fond smile. "This blade is called Zell. The rubies here are not merely for decoration. They are enchanted so that whenever this blade is in contact with demonic flesh and blood, it will unleash fire. When combined with your Heat spell, it will be devastating to your foes."

"Magnificent," said Gresten as he examined the blade.

Lady Silke knelt down and kissed Gresten on the forehead. He arose and in turn, kissed the back of her hand. He retrieved his, admittedly few, possessions and bowed before her once more.

"My red orb will show you the way towards your cousin's domain," said Lady Silke.

"My cousin?" asked Gresten.

"Second cousin once removed," replied Lady Silke. "The Tentacular Horror was once Duke Elton, King Gerath's second cousin. He was always a happy and well-meaning man, but the darkness in the city made him jealous. He wanted what King Gerath had and made a deal to become the ruler of Asmuth Swamp. Sadly, my power can now only

Jordan Allen

reach so far because of his influence. If you can kill him, I will resume my rightful place as the sole ruler of this mystical graveyard."

"I will see to it that this swamp is yours once more," said Gresten. The prince bowed once more and departed as Lady Silke delicately waved goodbye to him.

Gresten followed Lady Silke's red orb for hours, wading through muddy waters that almost reached the top of his boots and climbed through the overgrowth of the dense swamp. Much to his delight, there were no tricks and ruses to be had this time, which made the unpleasant trek much more bearable. Eventually, the red orb stopped moving and started to jitter.

"This is as far as my power can reach right now, Prince Gresten," came Lady Silke's voice. "Take care of yourself."

"And you, Lady Silke," the prince replied.

Gresten marched onwards by himself. He used his knife to scratch markings into the trees to show which way he had come from and which way he intended to go. He hoped that this would stop him from getting lost in the way that he had months previously. This part of the swamp was particularly soggy, so he wasn't expecting it to be an easy trek.

The prince dealt with muddy path after muddy path and bloated corpse after bloated corpse. It was exhausting, but he pushed on. His determination to see his promise to Sir Brand through and restore the honour of the Lochmeria family was absolute. He would let nothing get in his way, not challenging terrain and certainly not wicked demons, greater or lesser.

As night began to fall, Gresten stumbled upon an old, ruined tower. It was the perfect place to camp. He climbed to the top to survey the swamp. In the purple evening light, he could see the outline of Altburg to the east. It didn't look too far, perhaps a journey of a few hours should he take the right path. The rest of the swamp was a sea of trees, pools, and shrubbery. To the north, Gresten could see the mountains in the distance and to the south, he could see the plains that he had travelled across to reach the swamp.

Gresten climbed down and used the rubble to block the doorway. He dissipated his orb and lay on the floor. He thought about how he had hoped to be in and out of the city within a day or two. His journey so far had been almost four months. He smiled at the thought of his past naivety. Nobody he had met in Altburg or the lands close by had had the same attitude. They were all acutely aware of the trials and tribulations of such a wretched place.

The prince fell asleep while deep in his thoughts. He dreamed that he was riding his horse across the plains towards Altburg. He didn't stop to dismount this time; he trotted through the city gates. It was bustling with activity, and everybody looked normal. They bowed and waved to Gresten knowing that their prince was among the people. It was a nice dream.

Gresten awoke suddenly in the morning light to a woman's scream, followed by a man's deep yell. He didn't have time to grab his armour, only his sword, before throwing his barriers aside and rushing out.

A giant muddy brute covered in moss had grabbed a young woman while an armoured man attacked the beast with a mace. The towering filthy menace roared with fury as the man struck it, but it held the woman unrelentingly.

Gresten charged forward, hurling fireballs as he did so. The woman screamed again, thinking Gresten was attacking her, and the man turned to Gresten.

"Have you come to help or hurt?" he shouted while clashing with the twelve-foot-tall monster.

"Help you hurt this golem," called Gresten as he swung his sword at the hulk's leg, cleaving a chunk of its knee away only for it to reform from more mud.

"Well met," said the man as he returned his focus to the monster.

Gresten's blade did not glow as he struck the beast. Much like the corpses, this filthy brute was no demon. He would have to deal with it as he had done every other creature thus far.

The beast flailed wildly, shaking the woman, and kicking at the men by his legs. Both Gresten and the armoured man were knocked backwards. The man fell to the mud-covered ground, but Gresten reached a hand backwards and used his Push spell to force himself upwards before hitting the dirt.

The prince taunted the beast and circled around it, trying to draw it away from the man on the ground. Gresten focused once more, cleared his mind, and leapt at the beast. He used his Push to thrust himself a few feet higher, then grabbed onto the monster's neck with his free hand. He rammed Zell into the monster's gaping maw, and it let out a mighty roar as it fell backwards. It released the woman from its grip as it writhed in pain on the mud.

Gresten and the man both furiously hacked at the beast's limbs until it let out a final whimper before oozing back into the swamp floor. It left no trace, as though it was part of the swamp itself.

The man rushed to the woman, who had climbed back to her feet and was brushing off the debris from her robes. "Are you alright, Maiden Edith?"

"Yes," said the woman. "I'm fine thanks to you and this stranger."

The man turned to Gresten, removed his helmet and gave a bow. "I thank you for your aid in our time of need, stranger. Please enlighten us as to your name."

Gresten took a second to examine both of the individuals before him. The man looked to be in his mid-thirties with dark blonde hair, much darker than Gresten's, shaped in a bowl cut. He had a rough beard and was presumably clean-shaven before undertaking whatever journey he was on. He wore a blue tabard over his armour, and it bore the crest of a gryphon. The woman wore white robes with blue trim, also bearing a gryphon. She had long blonde hair, similar in colour to the man's, and had very delicate features. She couldn't have been as old as twenty yet.

Gresten gave a bow of his own. "My name is

Gresten. I'm a demon hunter from these parts."

The woman gave a deep bow before Gresten and moved her arms in an upwards motion as she did so. "Blessings of Koldur upon you, Gresten. My name is Maiden Edith of Warth and this is my guardian companion, Sir Otto of Warth."

Gresten knew Koldur to be a revered deity of the Outer World, the land of the living, who was often followed by nobles. Warth was an empire to the north, many hundreds of miles past the mountains he had seen from the tower. It had gathered many nations under its banner, but Lochmeria had never fallen to it. Gresten suspected that Warth would not want it anymore considering the current state of affairs in Altburg, the crown jewel of Lochmeria.

"You have come a long way from Warth, Maiden Edith. What brings you to such a wretched place as this?"

"We're seeking Duke Elton," interjected Sir Otto. "Maiden Edith received a vision from Koldur that told her she must purge him of his sin. He was a devout follower before...before he fell from grace."

"It's alright," said Gresten. "I know of his current predicament. I'm also seeking to kill the Tentacular Horror."

"Kill?" gasped Maiden Edith. "No, no! You mustn't. We're to save him from his sin and restore him to humanity."

"Is that still possible?" asked Gresten. Such a thing was unheard of to him.

"It is not only possible," said Sir Otto, "but we also come with the means to do so. We have brought all of the right implements for the ritual of cleansing and Maiden Edith is more than a skilled enough cleric to perform it."

"Will you help us?" pleaded Maiden Edith.

"I will," said Gresten without hesitation. It was worth trying. Perhaps if it worked, his father could be saved.

"I'm ever so pleased," smiled Maiden Edith with a small hop.

"Can I make a request?" asked Gresten.

"That depends on what the request is," said Sir Otto.

"If the ritual succeeds, I want you to help me purge a number of other demons in Altburg. I want them restored to humanity."

Chapter 8

The Ritual

"I cannot allow that," said Sir Otto. "We came here to deal with Duke Elton following Maiden Edith's vision from Koldur. No more, no less."

"No, Sir Otto," said Maiden Edith softly. "I will do it."

Sir Otto protested. "Maiden Edith, our mission."

"Our mission will be fulfilled upon saving Duke Elton. What we do after that is up to us. We have no set time to return to Warth and it would be most unbecoming of us to not help other tormented souls."

"Fine," Sir Otto relented. He was clearly still not happy about it.

"Thank you," said Gresten to both of them. "Please, come with me and rest a short while before we hunt for the horror."

Gresten led them back to the tower. While the priestess and the knight sat by the fire, Gresten cleaned his sword and put on his armour.

"How far did you travel to reach Altburg?"

Sir Otto chuckled. "It's been a long journey. We've travelled four hundred and seventy miles, give or take a few. We've been on the road for almost two months now."

"A far longer journey than mine to reach Altburg," said Gresten.

"Did you not say that you're from here?" asked Maiden Edith.

"Lochmeria, yes, but not Altburg. I've spent most of my life on the Isle of Green."

Sir Otto raised an eyebrow. "You share the name of one of the princes of Lochmeria. Did you know that?"

"I don't share the name, I am that prince," said Gresten. He trusted them enough to tell them, but it didn't seem like a particularly hard secret to figure out these days.

"What a bounty you would make," chortled Sir Otto while the priestess glared at him. "I'm joking, of course. We are not two nations at war, at least not presently."

"If we ever are, I'm sure we would have a fine duel," Gresten joked back. "I would win, of course."

"War is like the changing of the seasons," said Maiden Edith glumly. "It will always come back around until the world is nothing more than ash. While we are at peace, let us enjoy each other's company."

The three spent a few more minutes talking before departing from their oasis of mud and stone and venturing back into the heart of the swamp. The three battled more bloated corpses and swamp hulks along the way.

The young cleric was clearly skilled with magic, far more so than Gresten. She had been trained from childhood in the divine arts and it showed. Even after his months of training, Gresten had only a fraction of her abilities, but she wouldn't have lasted a second without a warrior like Sir Otto to protect her.

"Hold up," whispered Sir Otto. "What's that over there?"

The three crouched down in the reeds and looked to the pool that Otto gestured towards. There was a long tentacle protruding from the water and it was swaying back and forth as though in a trance.

"What should we do?" asked Maiden Edith.

"Throw a fireball," said Sir Otto looking at Gresten.

"Are you sure?" Gresten asked.

"No, but we can't reach it without magic unless we wade through the water."

He had a point, blunt as the idea may have been. Gresten conjured a fireball into the palm of his hand and threw it at the tentacle, striking it near the base. It swiftly retreated into the water and a loud, squelching shriek burst out from somewhere in the distance.

"We're getting close," said Gresten. "Perhaps that's a scout?"

"How large do you think the Tentacular Horror is?" asked Maiden Edith.

"Lady Silke advised that its body wasn't very large," said Gresten, "but its tentacles could be over fifty feet."

"Did she say if they detach?" asked Sir Otto.

"She did not," replied Gresten.

Gresten, Sir Otto and Maiden Edith stood up and walked in the direction of the shriek. They had a hunch that this was where they would find the body of the Tentacular Horror. As they came into another clearing with a large pool of water, they spied another tentacle protruding from the water.

"Cast your Fireball spell again," said Sir Otto.

"I want to try something else first," Gresten replied.

He brought his hand up and emitted a forceful Push across the water, knocking the tentacle backwards. It swayed and started thrashing wildly. It swam as though it were an eel towards the edge of the pool. It dragged itself towards the three, but Gresten threw a fireball at it. It thrashed some more, then shrivelled up. As the slimy tendril shrivelled, another shriek echoed in the swamp.

"This must be part of the Tentacular Horror," said Gresten. "Should we seek out more tentacles and kill them? Perhaps that will weaken him."

"Perhaps it will kill him if we take out too many," said Sir Otto. "No, I think we should only kill what we need to track the location of his cries."

"I agree, Sir Otto," said Maiden Edith. "Once we find him, I will prepare the ritual, but we must keep out of sight as it may take me a couple of minutes."

The trio proceeded deeper still into the swamp. The trees grew taller and the overgrowth thicker. Slowly lowering themselves down a slippery hill, Gresten tugged on the edge of Maiden Edith's robe.

"Quiet," he whispered while pointing to the largest pool so far at the bottom of the hill.

Inside the pool was a large, convoluted mass of tentacles. It was moving gently up and down as though taking breaths, all the while a large orange eye with a long black pupil darted around surveying the area. Gresten thought that attacking the tentacles may have been a mistake as the beast appeared to be very alert.

"Where to?" asked Sir Otto in a hushed voice.

Gresten gestured towards the pair to follow him, and he led them down the hill through the thickest part of the trees and shrubs. When they reached the bottom, they crawled behind a large mossy rock and breathed a sigh of relief. They appeared to not have been noticed so far.

"The ritual will start quietly, but I'm afraid the light will become visible quickly," uttered Maiden Edith in the quietest voice she could muster.

"I will head left, and Sir Otto will head right. When the light starts to show, we will cause whatever distractions we can to draw him away from you."

Sir Otto nodded in agreement.

"Good luck to both of you," said Maiden Edith with a sweet smile.

"And you Maiden Edith," smiled Gresten back.

"If things should go...poorly," said Sir Otto gingerly, "then know it has been an honour to serve as your guard, Maiden Edith."

Gresten kept low and moved left while Sir Otto took off to the right. There was something comforting about having travelling companions, but Gresten felt less vulnerable alone. The prince positioned himself behind a tree and waited. He could just about see the Tentacular Horror's eye moving rapidly.

After a minute of waiting, Gresten could see a faint glow behind the rock that Maiden Edith was waiting by. The prince picked up a clump of mud from the wet ground and readied his arm to throw it. Sir Otto was nowhere in sight, but Gresten expected he had done the same.

The Horror let out a sudden shriek, this time of anger, not pain. It rose its slimy mass of tentacles out of the water and moved towards Maiden Edith's rock. Gresten hurled a rock into the pool, but the Horror's sloshing was too loud, and it was unhindered.

"Oi!" yelled Sir Otto, emerging from behind a bush at the far side of the pool. He removed his helmet and started bashing it against his mace, making a loud clang that resonated across the pool.

The tentacled beast stopped and turned towards Sir Otto. He continued to make noise and it charged toward him. Gresten lobbed a fireball at the Horror while four of its tentacles whipped forward to grab Sir Otto. It shrieked and turned towards Gresten; its eye now fixated on him. It rose even taller out of the water and dislodged a dozen of its tentacles towards him and a dozen towards Sir Otto.

The separated tentacles shot through the water towards each man, while the body of the monster turned towards Maiden Edith. The priestess was now standing and chanting, both of her hands glowing while the light from her magic circle expanded wider.

Gresten threw a flurry of furious fireballs

rapidly at the charging tentacles, but he was not fast enough to stop them all. As they neared, he drew Zell, swinging the blade viciously to cut them to pieces.

Zell glowed orange and seared right through the tentacles. Gresten had always heard the tales of magical weapons forged from the essences of demons, dragons, and gods, but seeing one in action for the first time was a sight to behold even at a time like this.

Sir Otto let out a loud yell as he was flung into the water by one of the tentacles, vastly outnumbered by the slithering extensions of the Horror. Gresten was distracted for a split second, and one of the tentacles circled around his feet before tightening and tripping him up.

Gresten used his Heat spell, turning his glove red hot, then squeezed tight on the tentacle wrapped around his feet. The Horror shrieked once again in the distance as it continued towards Maiden Edith, the pain not enough to slow it down significantly. Gresten ran into the pool towards Sir Otto, who was being pulled beneath the surface by the tentacles. The water was only three feet deep, but they had pinned the knight down.

Gresten started slashing wildly, unable to see beneath the muddy waters. He prayed that he wouldn't hit Sir Otto. He had a sudden idea and summoned an Orb of Light, ordering it beneath the water. It lit up enough for Gresten to make out the silhouette of Sir Otto. The prince started stabbing the water around the knight, killing as many of the disgusting tentacles as possible to the screams of the Horror, then grabbed Sir Otto's arm to pull him to the surface.

Sir Otto gasped for air, "Maiden Edith," he said between breaths and both men charged towards the Tentacular Horror.

The demon was upon her, about to lunge down, but Gresten hurled another fireball through the air. It winced but proceeded to reach out with a tentacle. The tentacle pulled the priestess from her circle towards its body as she struggled to break free. The light faded and she disappeared from sight, pulled within the abominable mass.

Sir Otto let out a loud battle cry and dove within the creature himself. Gresten chased after, slashing at the tentacles on the back of the beast, determined to not let this be the fate of his newfound allies. With no other targets in sight, the demon turned to him and refocused its eye on the prince. It reached out a tentacle to pull the prince into it, where he would join Sir Otto and Maiden Edith, but the prince sliced the tentacle in half. The beast shrieked yet again and bent down towards him.

This was his chance. The prince drew Zell backwards and thrust it into the Horror's watchful eye. The demon let out a yell, more horrific than any so far and its tentacles started to melt away, steaming as they writhed, twisted and shrunk. As it shrivelled, Gresten could see Maiden Edith's hand inside the beast. He reached out to her and pulled her free, burning his hand on the acidic ooze that the beast was becoming. Maiden Edith had a few light burns to her skin, but she was alive, but there was no sign of Sir Otto. Knowing that the acidic beast would soon be the death of both him and Edith, he was forced to escape.

Gresten dragged the young Warthian through

the water to the edge of the pool while the Tentacular Horror dissolved into a steaming pile of ooze that spread throughout the pool. After a short while, one of Sir Otto's melted boots drifted to the surface before fully dissolving. The brave knight was no more, yet another victim of the prince's fallen kingdom.

Gresten let out a yell of anger. He threw Zell to the ground and fell to his knees. He had to act fast. He raised both of his hands to Maiden Edith and began casting his Healing Hands spell to repair her burns. He had only practised this on wounded animals and his own Lady Silke-inflicted injuries, but it had to work.

Slowly, Maiden Edith's skin healed as though new. She remained unconscious but mended. The prince threw her over his shoulder and marched away from the Tentacular Horror's pool. The demon was no more, but along with it, Duke Elton was dead.

Gresten marched his way back to his tower and scouted the quickest way back to the plains. It was a three-hour journey, but the prince continued to carry the unconscious Maiden Edith south until he exited the swamp. He did not rest until he reached the abandoned Runderside Inn where he had last met Reinhold.

*

Maiden Edith opened her eyes. She was in a rickety bed, and she felt very groggy. Sitting asleep on a chair beside her was the prince.

"Prince Gresten?" the priestess asked.

Gresten stirred from his sleep and smiled at her. "You're awake?"

"What happened?" asked the priestess, rubbing her eyes.

"I pulled you from the body of the Tentacular Horror and got you to safety. We're in a small inn outside of Altbug. You've been asleep for over a day."

"Sir Otto?"

Gresten lowered his head. "I'm sorry, but he didn't make it."

Maiden Edith sat up and wept. Gresten let her cry while he sat there silently until she eventually subsided.

"I'm sorry," said Maiden Edith. "I'm sorry I couldn't fulfil my part of the task. Koldur was wrong to give me this vision. I was not worthy."

"It was a tall ask," said Gresten. "I continually learn that, in this place, each time I try to do something I believe I'm capable of, I discover that I am not. It would have taken many more men to fend off the Horror while you cast your ritual. A luxury we simply don't have in Lochmeria these days."

"You were right," uttered the priestess. "We should have killed him from the start and Sir Otto would have survived."

"Maybe so, but maybe something else would not have worked out as intended."

Maiden Edith stood up, walked tepidly over to the window and looked outside. "It's so beautiful here. Why does this land suffer so?"

Gresten pondered. "This is our generation's test. This is our great tragedy."

"What about you?"

"Me?"

Maiden Edith looked at Gresten and nodded. "You're destined for greatness, so your life can't be easy. Can it?"

"I came here hoping to find the truth about what happened to my father, knowing in my heart already what the truth probably was. Now I've found myself focused on freeing my kingdom from the clutches of demonic occupation. I do not know that it is destiny, but I suppose you're right that my life can't be easy."

"Would you want it to be?" asked Maiden Edith.

"No," admitted Gresten. "No, I don't think I would want it to be easy. It's through great struggle that I'm discovering who I really am."

"Where will you go now?" asked Maiden Edith.

"There are two major demons still standing in my way before I face Za'gerath. The Fair Lady and the Bridge Guardian. I only know where the Bridge Guardian is, sadly."

Maiden Edith smiled at Gresten. "The Fair Lady is in the Sanctuary."

"The Sanctuary?" asked Gresten bewildered. "Where is that? How do you know this?"

"In Warth, we have more intelligence on your city than most of your citizens. Do you know the small forest outside the city walls to the west?"

"Yes, that's just a few miles south of here."

"There's a path up the cliffside that will lead you into the Sanctuary. It's one of the secret ways in and out of the city. If you go there, you'll find the Fair Lady."

"If she's still alive," said Gresten thinking of Hurm's intent to kill both the Fair Lady and the

Bridge Guardian. The more he had thought of this over the last few months, the more he was convinced that Hurm was simply trying to force him out of Altburg.

Gresten walked over to Maiden Edith. "Are you going to return to Warth?"

"I don't know if I would survive the journey alone," admitted Maiden Edith.

"Wait for me until I return from Altburg," said Gresten. "I will see to it that you're safe. I swear it, Maiden Edith."

Maiden Edith removed Gresten's left glove and took the prince's hand as they both watched the sunrise through the window.

Chapter 9

Sanctuary

Gresten walked along the cliffside path. It was finely carved from stone and no worse for the wear given its age. He looked to the west across the plains. It really was a beautiful kingdom. The farms and fields stretched out and the Runder weaved across the land, carving it into two intersecting pieces.

Maiden Edith had probably reached Hilda by now, Gresten thought to himself. He had instructed the fair priestess to stick to the roads to reach the gates of Altburg but to avoid the city at all costs. From there, she was to follow the road south to reach Hilda. She could then seek shelter in the nearest abandoned farmhouse until Gresten returned.

Returning from his thoughts, Gresten pushed

forward up the stone path. As he neared an archway in the cliffside, he spotted the skeletal remains of an unfortunate individual. It looked to be a young priest, based on the robes, and he had died just outside the entrance to the Sanctuary. A sad place to meet an end, especially when he was so close to freedom.

Gresten walked past the skeleton and into the dark archway. He cast the Orb of Light and proceeded cautiously down the stone tunnel. There were empty sconces spread out across the grey brick walls, but any flickering lights were long since gone. The only sounds the prince could hear outside of his own soft footsteps were the odd water droplets splashing onto the stone below and the occasional scurrying of a rodent.

What was that? Gresten stepped hurriedly back just as he was rounding the corner. He could have sworn he had seen a shadowy figure standing up ahead. He peered around the corner, but there was nothing in the tunnel ahead. It was empty.

The prince took a deep breath. He hadn't been in this tight of a space since the prison and it left him with a suffocating feeling. No matter. He must press on.

There was something there. Gresten stopped dead in his tracks again. He was certain he had seen something move up ahead. The prince squinted in the darkness trying to find it, but perhaps it was his own shadow on the wall ahead? Gresten watched as his orb floated around him and the shadow stayed still. If that were his shadow, thought the prince, then it should move around the room as the orb circled around him. No, something was watching him, and it knew that he was watching it too.

Gresten walked forward to the left, watching the shadow from the corner of his eyes. It stayed put. He softly raised his hand and sent a Push into the wall it rested on. It flinched and then fled upwards into the ceiling, scurrying along as though wispy smoke.

Gresten knew his sword would be of no use against a being without form and raised both of his hands ready to toss any spells he could at the shadowy creature. The shadow ran across the roof until it was directly above the prince, then it lunged out of the roof towards him, now corporeal. Gresten threw a fireball straight into its chest and the shadow demon burst into a cloud of smoke before dissipating.

The prince breathed a sigh of relief, but he knew that he would have to watch his steps like never before. At least he could avoid the bloated corpses of the swamp by taking certain paths, but the shadows could be anywhere around him, even above or beneath him. To lose sight of his surroundings was to meet his end.

The prince continued onwards, trying to find the right tunnel to take. These tunnels were filled with all sorts of crates, barrels, and pots, but more curiously were the rotted remains of the demon whelps. Was this one of the escape routes that people had taken when Altburg fell? It must have been based on the skeleton outside. Gresten would have been well beneath the city now, so it was the only theory that made sense to him.

Maiden Edith had told Gresten the rough layout of the tunnels as best as she could remember. Sadly, Sir Otto had possession of their map. The city was divided horizontally by the Runder, and he was looking to exit into an old guardhouse in the western section of the southern half.

Another sudden movement and a shadow on the wall froze as Gresten's gaze fell upon it. Gresten approached slowly hoping that it wouldn't realise he knew of its presence. He began to walk past it and readied a Fireball spell once more. The shadow's hand slowly emerged from the wall and Gresten could feel its fingers grab his shoulder. He launched the fireball at it, and it too exploded into smoke.

"Can I hurt them in the walls?" Gresten whispered under his breath. He wasn't sure if his Push spell had affected the first shadow, so he lured the second out. How fast were the reactions of the shadows? Would they be able to outpace the fire? It had to be tested.

A shadow in the tunnel ahead. It walked slowly towards Gresten, already outside of the walls. Gresten readied a fireball.

"I would prefer you not to hit me with that," came a voice.

"Hurm?" whispered Gresten.

As the figure approached, Gresten recognised the wooden mask with the tusks. It was indeed Hurm.

"Why are you back here?" asked Hurm.

"What are you doing down here?" asked

Gresten.

"Answer me first, then I'll answer you."

"I've taken care of the Foreman and the Tentacular Horror, as agreed. Have you already dealt with the Fair Lady and the Bridge Guardian?"

"It's been months. I thought you had come to your senses and escaped."

"So, you did send me as far as possible in the hopes I wouldn't return. Why?"

"I already told you why," said Hurm angrily.

Gresten was equally angry. "What concern of yours is it that I'm kept alive? Who is my mother to you?"

"It matters not. All that matters is that I made her a promise and I wanted to make sure it was kept. I thought you would leave through the caves, then be gone for good. It's why I sent word ahead to Horban of Roch. He was there to keep you safe."

"You sent Horban? He knew all this time?"

"No," said Hurm, "all he knew was that there was somebody that could help him with his own hunt and that you would try and make a deal with him. I encouraged him to accept."

"Horban died helping me kill the Foreman."

"I'm aware of that, Prince. Do not think that I am pleased about this in any way."

"What of the Fair Lady and the Bridge Guardian?" asked Gresten again.

Hurm didn't speak for a moment. "I cannot kill them, nor any of the other greater demons."

"Why?" asked Gresten. "You're clearly skilled."

"I cannot kill them, I cannot physically attack them, and they will make no attempts to attack me."

"Why?" asked Gresten again.

"Because I am cursed," said Hurm. "I'm cursed to live in this city until my dying day. To the stronger of the demons, I am but a phantom. To me, they are phantoms. There is nothing I can do. I've given up on fighting with the lesser demons because their numbers are seemingly endless. The joke is that the curse was intended to protect me from Za'gerath, but it imprisoned me in ways you cannot possibly imagine."

"I'm sorry to hear that you are afflicted with this curse," said Gresten softly.

"I have made my peace with it," said Hurm. "Now please do as I ask and return to the Isle of Green."

Hurm turned his back on Gresten and walked back down the tunnel.

"How did you know I was here?" Gresten called after him.

Hurm didn't answer and faded into the shadows ahead.

Gresten presumed Hurm would try to lead him in a circle and back to the exit, so he proceeded down a different tunnel. He kept his eyes on the walls, the ground, and the ceiling. If the shadows could hear, they would hear Gresten. He also had yet to see any sign of the Fair Lady.

A sudden movement from a shadow. It froze when Gresten turned to see it. The enigmatic figure stared straight at him from the wall to his right. Gresten threw a small fireball at it, but it did not flinch. He tapped on the wall with Zell, but it still did not flinch. He cast a Push spell at it, then the creature lunged for him. Gresten fell backwards and thrust Zell upwards into the heart of the demon. Zell lit up with intense heat and the shadow burst silently into a cloud of smoke.

Divine magic. That was the key to drawing out the shadows, then fire can kill them. Perhaps if the Fair Lady was like these creatures, it would work on her too?

Gresten could hear the scraping of metal on the floor up ahead. He froze in his tracks and lowered the light of his orb. He leaned around the corner into the next room and saw a woman standing in the centre, with her head in her hands. She appeared to be sobbing.

Gresten was not going to fall for this. That must be her, the Fair Lady. Gresten stepped quietly out and raised his hand to knock her down, but she turned to face him. She screamed and then ran down a tunnel with the scraping metal sound following her.

The prince turned up his light and looked frantically around. There were shadows leaping from the walls surrounding him. He drew Zell and threw a flurry of fire around himself while spinning Zell through the air. The bursts of smoke covered Gresten's light. He was blind in this room.

Gresten could feel the shadowy hands wrap their spindly fingers around his limbs. He focused and cast Heat on his armour. The fingers recoiled and Gresten stabbed at them wildly in the dark.

A woman's voice called out from the darkness. "Are you not afraid? Please, let me ease your

suffering."

"I am not afraid of you," yelled Gresten as he continued to stab at the shadows grabbing between the gaps in his armour. The smoke thickened.

"I am only here to help, Gresten. Please, let me heal you," said the woman. She sounded sincere, but Gresten knew this was part of the ruse.

Gresten stabbed in front of him and charged ahead toward the voice. His orb followed and he could see once more. The shadows began to close in around him again, but he ignored them and followed the woman's voice in the tunnel.

The woman floated slowly towards him and Gresten knocked her down with a push. She floated straight back up again.

"You need me, my prince," said the Fair Lady. "I will heal you so you can heal this kingdom."

"Your lies will not work on me, demon," called Gresten as he drew Zell up to his eye line and pointed it forward.

The prince charged straight into the woman, casting Heat on his armour once again so the woman would be unable to touch him. It hurt badly, but he ran straight through her ghostlike figure, and she screamed in pain as he did so. While she gathered herself, Gresten stabbed her with Zell.

The Fair Lady cried out in agony. "Why? I am only here to help. I must heal! It is my duty."

The shadows following Gresten backed off and sank back into the walls as the Fair Lady began emitting white smoke. She withered and fell to the ground, her flesh melting, leaving nothing but a singed robe on the stone. Her cries faded into nothing and the robe slowly disappeared from sight.

That trick may have worked on a fleeing civilian a year ago, but Gresten would not fall for it. Anybody who wanted to leave Altburg was either dead or had left already.

Gresten suspected that the shadows would not bother him again, but he was cautious regardless. Continuing down the tunnel was much more peaceful now. He reached a large chamber that contained a ladder. Perhaps this was the exit he sought?

"You are persistent," came Hurm's voice from the corner of the room.

Gresten turned to face him. "Yes."

"I am surprised she fell to you so easily."

"Her methods rely on trickery, but she is frail. If the trickery fails, so too does she."

Hurm nodded understandingly. "Do you want to see why this place was called the Sanctuary?"

"Show me," said Gresten.

Hurm beckoned him forwards and led Gresten down a series of tunnels. Suddenly, the underground tunnels opened up into what looked to be a small town. Light trickled in from the gratings above and Gresten could see houses and shacks scattered throughout this large chamber. It was a surprising sight.

"What is this place?" asked the prince.

"This was the Sanctuary," said Hurm. "The rest of the tunnels were simply tunnels out of the city and extra storage, but this spot was the original Sanctuary before everything down here became known as the Sanctuary."

"Did the Fair Lady come from here?"

"In a manner of speaking. She's unlike the other greater demons that you've faced before. She was here before Za'gerath."

"How so?" asked Gresten.

"Sister Margaret was a priestess of the True One who worked down here treating the sick. This was a large camp for the homeless of the city and she was dedicated to them. She would tell people of the greatest healer priestess to ever have lived, Sister Miriam. Sister Margaret would always comfort the dying by saying that Sister Miriam would come and treat them. When Sister Margaret herself was dying, she became delirious. She unwittingly made a deal with a demon and her imaginary creation, Sister Miriam, was given physical form. The Fair Lady."

"Did people not know of this demon haunting these tunnels?"

"The Fair Lady was a demon, but she was mostly harmless. She was always chained to the floor by phantom shackles, but when Za'gerath's influence spread, she became unshackled and dangerous. She would devour her victim's soul first, then the flesh, then the bones."

"I saw a skeleton outside."

"That lucky skeleton probably died just outside of the Sanctuary. She could not leave these tunnels."

"Now she's gone," said Gresten.

"Indeed, she is," Hurm said. Gresten could tell Hurm had smirked beneath his mask.

"Was what you told me true?" asked Gresten.

"Which part?"

"That if the four greater demons are killed, Za'gerath would weaken?"

"I did not say that at all," said Hurm.

"You did," insisted Gresten.

"No, I told you that his influence would weaken. I said nothing about his strength weakening, nor that there were only four of these powerful demons. You seem to have heard what you wanted to hear, not what I said."

"All of this was for nought?"

"For nought? I suggest you rethink, prince. Have you saved any lives? Whether that's present lives or lives that won't be lost to these monsters. Have you gotten stronger? You would not have survived these tunnels had you not been training in your magic. I presume you met Lady Silke in the graveyard swamp?"

"You're right," said Gresten, relenting. "Of course, you're right. It was foolish for me to have suggested my time here was for nought."

"You're going to continue to the Bridge Guardian above?" asked Hurm.

"Yes, I am."

"Very well. I will not stop you, but I will be of no use to you. Perhaps we will meet again, perhaps not. I wish you all the blessings I have left, Prince Gresten."

Hurm turned around and walked back down the tunnel.

"I wish you all the best too, Prince Germund," said Gresten.

Hurm paused but did not look back before continuing to walk away.

Chapter 10

A True Blessing

Gresten leaned out of the guardhouse and looked down the street. There were a few straggling whelps, but they would no longer be of the slightest threat to Gresten without the help of stronger demons beside them. He knew this area from before. He wasn't too far from Saint Rudolph's church.

The prince navigated the streets, remembering them from a more sheltered part of his life a mere four months ago. It had not been long, but it felt like a lifetime ago. Gresten effortlessly cut down the whelps with Zell as they approached. Each dead demon was one that would never hurt another soul again. He could not hope to kill everything in the city this simply, but it was a start.

The church was ahead of Gresten once more. He walked up to the doors and entered, ensuring to close them behind himself. Saint Rudolph was bowed down in prayer by the altar, so Gresten sat quietly a few feet away to let the priest focus.

"I'm pleased to see that you are back," said Saint Rudolph, turning to Gresten with a caring smile on his face. "You look weathered, young prince. Weathered, but strong."

"Thank you, Saint Rudolph," said Gresten standing up, then kneeling with his head bowed. "I would not be here were it not for your previous hospitality and training. A spell as simple as Push has saved me many times over."

"I thought it would be of assistance to you, young prince. It is among the most basic of spells, but that can often be the most effective."

Saint Rudolph walked over to the aisle and sat down, gesturing for Gresten to sit down beside him. Gresten arose from his kneeling position and sat.

"What brings you back here, my son?" asked the saint.

"I do not plan to stay long. I wanted to make sure that you were okay and then to thank you."

"I am more than fine. I am very grateful to the True One to see you alive and well. I had heard through the grapevine that you were imprisoned."

"Through the grapevine?"

"Word travels fast even in a city with no people."

Gresten remained puzzled and Saint Rudolph chuckled at his expression. "Wagner heard it from a man in the prison, but he had not heard any updates in a few months. Contact with prisoners is difficult."

"I've been in the prison, I've been in the Caves of Cavaurus, I've been in Asmuth Swamp, and I've been in the Sanctuary. It's been quite a journey."

Gresten told his story, in great detail, to Saint Rudolph. If the prince could be honest about everything with anybody, it was him. The whole time, Saint Rudolph stayed silent while listening to the story.

"That's everything, your reverence," concluded Gresten.

"That is quite the adventure you've had, young prince," said Saint Rudolph. "You truly believe that Hurm is your brother?"

"I do."

"I cannot say that I know him well, but we have met. He has never removed his mask in my presence, so it is entirely possible that he is Prince Germund."

Gresten nodded in silent agreement.

"This Reinhold you speak of," Saint Rudolph continued. "He never revealed his face to you, nor his full name?"

"No, he did not. Do you think he could be my brother?"

"No, he is not. His full name is Reinhold Lochmeria. He is your first cousin. Your father's brother's bastard son. You suspect something is off about him, you say? I suspect that it's because he knows who you are now. Reinhold made it his mission when he arrived here to kill Za'gerath personally and he likely suspects that you'll try to do it first. He wants the glory. Be careful around him. I do not believe him to be a bad man, but I do believe him to be ambitious to a fault."

Gresten contemplated what he had just heard. It made a lot of sense after his last interaction with Reinhold and explained why things were so tense.

"I'm expecting Master Wagner along this evening with more supplies," said the saint.

Saint Rudolph and Gresten talked a while more before Gresten joined the saint in a few prayers. The prince had ensured that he prayed regularly, even while training with Lady Silke. She was not a follower of the True One like he, but she usually left him to it.

"Saint Rudolph," called Wagner as he burst through the door.

"Yes, Master Wagner?"

"I've received word that Prince Gres—"

Wagner stopped once he spotted Gresten kneeling by the altar. The prince arose and walked down the steps to greet Wagner.

"It is good to see you, sire," said Wagner.

"And you, Master Wagner," said the prince, giving Wagner a courteous nod.

"I had heard from Alvaro that you were long gone from the city."

"Alvaro knew who I was? I had been very careful not to tell him my name."

"I don't believe he knew who you were, but he described you and I was able to work it out."

Saint Rudolph shook his head. "Alvaro is no good. I do not know why you continue to risk associating with him, Master Wagner."

Wagner looked uneasy. "I know he's a vile fellow, your reverence, but he's an excellent source of information in the city if you toss him a coin."

Gresten stared at Wagner with thoughts of his friend Horban's death running through his head. Gresten had known Horban for only a few hours, but the Rochian had left an impact on the prince.

"You've had a run-in with him?" asked Wagner

with an uncomfortable look on his face.

"He killed a friend of mine before attempting to kill me," said Gresten. He could not hide the contempt in his voice, nor did he want to. The prince explained everything about his time in the mines to Wagner.

"I'm sorry to hear all of that, sire," said Wagner sincerely.

"I urge you to be wary, Master Wagner," said Saint Rudolph.

"If you can point me in the worm's direction," urged the prince, "I would be more than happy to take care of him."

"I'm afraid that Alvaro is already dead," said Wagner. "That man has made it out of some of the most slippery situations imaginable and lived to tell the tale, but his greed got the better of him in the end."

"What happened?" asked Gresten.

"A bounty hunter took him out."

"Eburhard?" asked Saint Rudolph with a slight cock of the head.

Wagner nodded. "Eburhard. I'm not sure of the full details, but Eburhard is a fearsome warrior when he's got a bounty. Don't get me wrong, he's friendly on the surface, but you don't want to get on his bad side."

"I do not like to speak ill of the dead, but I am not saddened by this news," admitted Gresten. The room went quiet for a while.

Saint Rudolph was the first to speak, breaking the silence. "I think that we should move on from this rather unpleasant topic and enjoy a nice meal together before you both take off into the streets again.

The three men ate a dinner of cooked pigeon and bread. Afterwards they enjoyed a couple of fresh apples that Wagner had retrieved from the same forest that Gresten had swam to after escaping the prison.

Gresten told Wagner of his tale and Wagner spoke of his own adventures in Altburg. The prince had seen the maps and walked the streets, but he never quite fathomed how big Altburg was. Even during his earlier travels, he had never been past the Runder to the north side of the city. He had only been to small parts of the southern half of the city and the prison on the central island.

"You should see some of the secrets this city holds, sire," said Wagner. "The houses near us right now are mostly for the common folks, but some of the old elite at the north had their own manors with large swathes of land. You would not expect it if you've only seen the tightly packed streets in this district. The traps, both mechanical and magical, that secure their treasures are more dangerous than almost any demon."

"I will be sure to avoid it at all costs then," laughed Gresten. "I have a good grasp on most of the demons here at this stage and I don't wish to test my fortune beyond that."

"That's fair," chuckled Wagner.

"I have a question plaguing my mind that one of you may be able to answer," began Gresten. "Why is it that the city fell so easily? Altburg was home to some of the most valiant knights and powerful wizards. Did nobody fight?"

Saint Rudolph bowed his head. "Za'gerath played a long game, Prince Gresten. He had driven the best and brightest from the city. As the city was corrupted from the top, it trickled down throughout the ranks. The most capable chose to leave and many others met unfortunate ends before that. By the time the assault was launched on Altburg, nobody was willing to fight for what it had become."

"It is sad," said Wagner. "I am originally from a town in southern Lochmeria. There were many who left Altburg over the years and settled in the surrounding lands, including my home. We sympathised with them and took them in, not realising the extent of the damage done to the city. Silent invaders and parasites sucked on the blood of this city and left it a husk, leaving the citizens to become strangers in their own country."

Gresten was sheltered from most of this on the Isle of Green. It was a small island of no more than two hundred inhabitants. A few dozen in the fort where Gresten, his mother and their servants had resided with mostly farmers, fishermen and their families living elsewhere on the island.

Gresten retired to the floor shortly after dinner, weary after his battles in the Sanctuary earlier that day. It was a pleasant evening of peace after such a trying time since departing from Lady Silke's home. The prince slept soundly on the stone and had a dreamless night for the first time in a long time.

*

In the early morning, Gresten prepared to depart from Saint Rudolph's church once more. As the prince began saying his goodbyes to both Wagner and Saint Rudolph, the saint halted him.

"I will give you a blessing once again, Prince Gresten. This is the most powerful blessing I can offer you. You will not notice what it does, at first, but I promise that it will help. Please kneel down by the altar."

Gresten walked to the altar and kneeled as he was asked. Saint Rudolph stood in front of him and began to pray. The saint's hands glowed a warm golden colour and he placed them on Gresten's temples. Gresten felt a slight static, but he was at peace.

"That should do it," said Saint Rudolph. "Do not ask what it does, just know that it will help you."

"I appreciate everything you've done for me, your reverence," said Gresten, on his feet again. "Your wise words, your kindness, and your faith in the True One has created a beacon of hope for stragglers like me. I only hope that someday I can repay you."

"Your success so far at ridding Altburg of evil is payment enough. I only ask that you see through what you started."

Wagner walked over to the prince. "I wish you the best of luck, once again, sire. I know for certain that the Bridge Guardian will pose no threat to you this time. You have grown powerful over the last few months. I can see it written on your face."

"Thank you, Master Wagner," said Gresten. "I'm sure we will meet again soon."

Gresten gave his final farewells to both and departed from the church for the second time. It felt familiar, yet new. When he had left the first time, he was seeking answers to the questions he had about his father. This time the prince left with a stronger sense of duty to his kingdom. A stronger sense of duty to his people. He was determined to not let those who had helped him along the way down. He would fulfil his promise to Sir Brand and Altburg would be reclaimed.

Chapter 11

Crossing the Bridge

Gresten walked through the streets of Altburg, slaying many whelps along the way. He no longer felt unsafe in the city, rather he felt vengeful. It would be reclaimed in the name of Lochmeria once more and it would be by his hand, the hand of a true Lochmerian.

Halfway to his destination, a man in heavy black plate with gold trim came into view along the main road. He walked towards the prince, raising a hand to signal that he was not a demon and lifted the grill of his helmet.

"Did you come from Saint Rudolph's church?" enquired the man. "That is my destination as we speak. My name is Eburhard."

"Well met, Eburhard," said Gresten. "I have heard of you from Master Wagner. I believe I should be thanking you."

"What for?" asked Eburhard, visibly confused.

"Alvaro the Worm," said Gresten. "I've heard he had a bounty on his head, and you took care of him. Is that not the case?"

Eburhard chuckled. "Truth be told, lad, he did it to himself. I still collected the bounty anyway."

"What happened?" asked Gresten.

"He was hauling some of his latest finds to his hideaway, while he was being chased by whelps. He was too greedy to let go of the goods, and he tripped. The whelps started tearing into him and the poor worm was no more. Got what he deserved if you ask me."

"I should say so," said Gresten. "Who placed the bounty?"

Eburhard scratched his nose. "Alvaro had plenty of enemies. He made them no matter where he went. I'm sure that's no surprise to you if you've met him."

"That is not a surprise at all," said Gresten. The prince was unsure why Eburhard was so evasive with his answer, but Gresten did not want to make an enemy of him. "I must be going while the road ahead is free of demons. I wish you a safe journey to the church."

"Careful up ahead, my friend. There's a blackguard skulking around up there. I tend to avoid them if I can help it."

"Thank you, Master Eburhard. Take care."

"And you, stranger," said Eburhard as he pulled his grill down. He walked down a side street and out of view.

Gresten couldn't shake the feeling that there was something not quite right about Eburhard's tale of Alvaro's fate. He could not rationalise it; it was a feeling in his gut that told him there was more to the story. Pushing aside his doubts, the prince carried on.

Gresten had longed to fight a blackguard after his last abysmal failure. A lesser demon than some that he had slain recently, but he felt as though he had something to prove to himself. It was a measure of progress now that he was so swiftly eliminating whelps.

Around the next corner was the blackguard, as Eburhard had warned. It stood rigidly upright in its black plate armour with its glowing red eyes, protruding horns, and gothic mace. The blackguard charged towards Gresten who drew Zell and readied himself.

The demon dragged its mace along the stone and swung it upwards as it reached the prince. Gresten blocked with Zell. It was a powerful strike, but he was prepared. Gresten cast a Push spell on the blackguard's leg, and the demon slipped forwards to the ground. Gresten could not see a clean opening in the armour from this angle, so he cut off one of the demon's horns with a heavy strike. The remaining stump steamed where Zell had struck.

The blackguard rolled out of the way of a further attack and climbed to its feet. It looked toward Gresten and spat a stream of acid at him. Gresten instinctively raised his hand and cast Push. The acid splashed back at the blackguard and burned its face beneath its helmet.

Gresten ran forward with Zell raised, as the blackguard roared in pain. The prince thrust Zell through the opening of the demon's helmet and kicked it back. It collapsed onto the cobblestones in a heap. Satisfied, at last, Gresten pressed on.

Arriving at the bridge once more, Gresten stood and pondered. The Bridge Guardian was not visible from the archway, but Gresten knew he would be there waiting. That was his sole purpose. The prince wondered what the demon would do should the bridge ever collapse.

"We meet again," came the voice of Reinhold from behind.

"We do indeed, Reinhold Lochmeria," said Gresten without looking around.

Reinhold laughed. "Our fates appear to be intertwined, Gresten Lochmeria. Perhaps it is because we are family and that is simply the way of things?"

"I had wondered if I would find out your fate by seeing whether the Bridge Guardian was still here or not."

"I have made a few attempts at crossing, I will admit, but none of them fruitful," said Reinhold.

Gresten could tell there was more to that story, much like with Eburhard, but did not push further. He needed Reinhold to help fight the Bridge Guardian. "Shall we resume where we left off four months ago?"

"Yes, I think so," said Reinhold. "We have plenty to discuss after we kill him. I daresay you think the same."

"I do," said Gresten.

The two men walked through the archway side by side and began their journey across the bridge. The atmosphere was tense between them with neither man saying a word. They were focused on the task at hand and that was enough for now. Any conversation was a distraction.

The Bridge Guardian came into view quickly and Reinhold raised his shield, ready to defend. As the men approached, the behemoth stirred and walked forward with his hammer-like fists raised, much as he had done many moons ago.

"Do not get hit this time," said Gresten jokingly.

"I won't," said Reinhold sternly.

Reinhold ran forward and the Bridge Guardian swung at him. Reinhold stepped aside, dodging the attack, while Gresten ran between its legs. The prince stabbed between the gaps in its stone armour, hoping Zell would take care of the rest, but even with Zell's enchantment the titan remained standing, so large and sturdy was this enormous demon.

The two men weaved in and out, dodging the fists of the Bridge Guardian that crashed into the bridge like giant boulders. The duo flanked him to keep his attention split. During the chaos, Reinhold's sword struck a small gap in the creature's knee armour and it lost its balance, staggering and leaving itself open, but dropping a hand to steady itself upon the bridge. Gresten rolled aside and used his Push to prevent the titan's fist from crushing him to a bloody, royal paste.

Gresten quickly clambered onto the crouching demon's back as Reinhold delivered a flurry of slashes to the weak points in its legs. As the behemoth climbed to its feet, Gresten clung to its neck. The Bridge Guardian swung its huge fists behind it, trying to hit Gresten, but the prince held tight and used his Heat spell on its rough flesh.

The colossus started thrashing ever more

rapidly as the prince clung to it. Swinging and writhing as it was, the prince remained steadfast and refused to relinquish his grip. Reinhold stepped back to avoid becoming collateral damage as the stomping Bridge Guardian continued its wild flailing.

Gresten held on tight with one hand and raised Zell with the other. He drew the blade back and, with an almighty thrust, he shoved it deep inside the Bridge Guardian's helmet. Unable to scream, it threw up its arms in agony as the magic of Zell's holy enchantment flowed through its head and coursed into the rest of its body. The brute fell backwards and Gresten leapt off of it onto the bridge below. He nearly stumbled off the edge but managed to steady himself, breathing a sigh of relief at conquering the foe that had once given him so much trouble.

The towering demon lay dead before Gresten and Reinhold. At last.

"We did it," said Gresten as he held out his hand to Reinhold.

Reinhold moved as though to grab Gresten's hand but suddenly kicked him backwards. Reinhold dove forward and shoved Gresten off the bridge, but Gresten sent a Push backwards into the air to right himself and knocked Reinhold aside with a mighty shove.

Gresten created some distance between him and his opponent, unsure why Reinhold just tried to kill him. "Explain yourself," demanded the prince.

"No," said Reinhold as he raised his shield. It began to glow a deep blue.

"Don't you owe me that? We're family."

"It's precisely because we're family that you can't live. I waited months for you to return here. I was starting to wonder if you were dead."

"You didn't try to kill the Bridge Guardian at all, did you? You were hoping it would kill me and you would be there to make sure it did."

"The throne of Lochmeria will be mine!" screamed Reinhold.

"I did not come for the throne," insisted Gresten. "I came to find out the truth about Za'gerath, but now I only want to see him dead and the kingdom delivered back to the people of this land."

Reinhold was too angry to listen and charged forward. Gresten cast Push to knock his shield aside, but whatever enchantment was on it blocked Gresten's spell. Gresten and Reinhold's swords collided, and the two men duelled.

Gresten swung and Reinhold blocked with his shield, following up with a swing of his own sword. Gresten used his magic to push the blade aside, then delivered a counterattack to Reinhold, who swiftly moved aside. The two fought vigorously, neither willing to concede an inch, even with Gresten's reluctance to deliver a killing blow.

The prince tried to cast his spells, but Reinhold was fast enough to dodge or block with his shield. He seemed far more skilled than he had done months ago, but perhaps an opponent his own size was what he knew best.

Reinhold stepped backwards, creating a gap between the prince and himself, and then raised his hand. A magic circle appeared on the bridge, glowing a deep red before a demon whelp rose from within. Reinhold was using infernal magic;

the same magic Lady Silke had forbidden Gresten from being taught because of its corruptive nature. Gresten knew that Reinhold was no longer in his right mind. He was beyond reason.

Gresten cut down the whelp and Reinhold summoned three more. They all charged at once and Reinhold used Gresten's killing of them as a distraction to land a devastating blow to Gresten's side. Gresten fell to the ground, clinging tightly to his sword, fearing that losing his weapon would mean losing the battle, and thus, his life.

Reinhold charged in once again and Gresten parried his attack, rolling backwards and jumping to his feet as he ignored the pain of Reinhold's previous attack. The angered Lochmerian swung with his full weight and Gresten's blade met his own. They were locked together, trying to force each other back.

With no other options, Gresten cast Push on Reinhold's sword, freeing it from its master's grip and sending it soaring over the edge of the bridge. Reinhold had no weapon, but he still had his shield and Gresten knew he needed that gone next.

The prince forced Reinhold's shield arm aside with Zell and knocked his angered cousin back with a kick. Gresten wrestled the shield from Reinhold and tossed it over the edge of the bridge, into the water below where it joined Reinhold's sword.

"I will not allow you to kill me!" yelled Reinhold with rage in a deep voice, unlike his own. He screamed a bloody scream and two horns erupted from within his helmet. He conjured a flaming sword in his hand and charged at Gresten.

Gresten raised his own sword, cast Heat, and

clashed with Reinhold once more. Reinhold was stronger than before and began pushing Gresten back towards the edge of the bridge. Gresten could not risk letting go of Zell to cast another spell. Reinhold pushed him up against the low wall and loosened his pressure ever so slightly to strike Gresten once more, wanting the prince dead immediately.

This was Gresten's chance. He grabbed Reinhold's helmet with one of his hands and cast Heat again. Reinhold screamed in agony as his black helmet glowed orange. Gresten pulled his helmet off, seeing Reinhold's face for the first time, and cut his head from his body. Reinhold's corpse buckled and fell backwards.

Gresten dropped to his knees, utterly exhausted, and let out a yell of his own. He was saddened by Reinhold's death, even more saddened that he was the one who had to kill him. This city and its corruption had spread too far and permeated so deeply. It needed to be stopped and it would be stopped today.

The prince looked down at Reinhold. Gresten could see the resemblance between Reinhold and himself, albeit Reinhold was older and longer in the face. Gresten couldn't help but wonder if his initial dishonesty with Reinhold played a part in his growing jealousy and resentment. If Gresten had been forthright with his cousin in the first place, perhaps Reinhold wouldn't have fallen to the corrupted Altburg and the devastation of Za'gerath's influence.

As he contemplated this, Gresten finally began to understand why the Bridge Guardian, the Foreman and the Tentacular Horror became what they were. The anger and resentment built up in the evil-infested city and they aligned with malevolent forces to keep up with whatever they thought was slipping away from them. Had Reinhold sold his soul while waiting for Gresten or did he sell it to survive the fall from the bridge? Gresten knew that he would never know the answer, but the question played on his mind.

Gresten picked up Reinhold's body and threw it into the river below. Gresten knelt and said a prayer, hoping that whatever was left of Reinhold's soul was not being sent to one of the hells. He prayed that an inkling of his newfound cousin would reach the Inner World, but he knew that this hope was in vain.

Gresten gathered himself and walked down the bridge. He knew there would be wardens waiting for him. The fat demons approached the prince from the stairs to the castle as he walked towards them, but he hurled a flurry of fireballs at them, in no mood for a drawn-out duel with his former captors. The pair of wardens fell quickly and Gresten marched up the stairs.

The prince was ready to face Za'gerath. He was ready to face what was left of his father.

Chapter 12

Bow to the King

Gresten flung open the castle doors. The white and black chequered tiles stretched out before him, adorned with a long red carpet. The edges of the room were filled with ornate vases, painted pots, and dusty suits of armour. On the walls throughout the entrance hall were magnificent portraits of members of the royal family, new and old. Gresten spotted a portrait of a pair of twin blonde boys who looked to be about two years old. The plaque beneath read, "Gresten Lochmeria, Germund Lochmeria."

Memories of the castle from twenty years prior came flooding back to Gresten. He knew exactly where he would end up if he walked down the left corridor, the staircase to the right, etc. He thought he was finally home when he arrived in Altburg, but he was finally home when he walked into the castle.

"You've made it," came Hurm's voice from the shadows on the staircase.

"I have," replied Gresten.

"Do you remember the way to the chamber with the balcony? That's where Za'gerath often spends his time. He watches over the city enjoying the spectacle that he's created. I do not doubt that he already knows of your acts."

"I think I remember, yes. It's the strange room where you have to go to the far side of the castle, up the stairs and then circle back on yourself on an upper floor, right?"

"That's the one," said Hurm as he rose and walked further back into the shadows.

"If you're only a phantom to Za'gerath," began Gresten, "then why don't you come with me?"

Hurm stopped in place. "I cannot watch you die and see my promise to our mother broken. I'm certain that's what will happen, brother."

Hurm faded into the shadows of the stairway leaving Gresten standing in the entrance hall alone. He had believed that Hurm was Germund for a short while, but it was nice to hear him admit it.

The prince walked down the corridor ahead. The frosted glass windows on both sides let the morning light in, casting a colourful dancing pattern on the floor. Gresten could see a blackguard further down the corridor waiting for him.

Gresten raised Zell and beckoned the blackguard forwards. The demon fell for his taunt and charged at him, readying its mace. Gresten cast Push on its arm as it swung the mace at him, tossing the mace aside. As the demon staggered, Gresten thrust Zell inside its helmet, killing the blackguard instantly.

Proceeding further into the castle, Gresten took a few moments to peer into every room. If he would not make it out alive, he would like to remember his childhood. He wanted to see the rooms that he would play in with his brother, the rooms he would be given lectures in by his father, and the rooms he would be comforted in by his mother. It brought him some peace in this hellscape.

Gresten reached the staircase he sought and walked to the top. As he stepped through the doorway, he found himself in...the entrance hall. No, that wasn't right. The prince looked backwards and, true enough, the doors to the castle that he stepped through minutes before were behind him once more.

Gresten ran ahead and found the blackguard he had already killed still lying dead in the corridor. He ran up the staircase, through the doorway and...he was in the entrance hall for the third time. What sorcery was this? The school of infernal magic was filled with illusions, warping of reality and the desire for control. This was no doubt Za'gerath's handiwork so that he could not be found easily. Germund must have known already. Perhaps he hoped that if Gresten could not find Za'gerath then he would finally give up. No, Gresten would not give up after everything he had been through.

Gresten climbed each staircase in the entrance hall to try and reach another floor of the castle, but each time he stepped through a doorway or an archway he was transported straight back to the entrance hall. Curiously, the rooms themselves were unaffected. Perhaps the secret was in one of the rooms?

The prince walked into every room he could find and examined them thoroughly. It felt silly, but he even looked under the tables, in the cupboards and lifted the carpets hoping to see some sort of hidden doorway or portal.

"This painting," said Gresten to himself in the lower kitchen. "Why is it a painting of a corridor? Is this another part of the castle?"

Gresten walked up to the painting and touched it. He watched his hand pass through the canvas, but there was no resistance or tear. This must be it. Gresten climbed inside the painting and finally found himself upstairs. It was not the exit he wanted to arrive at, but it was progress.

The prince was suddenly knocked to the floor by a powerful blow. He rolled to the side and saw a blackguard readying another strike, so Gresten blocked with Zell. He kicked the blackguard's leg and stood up while it collected itself. The prince threw fireballs at the opening in the demon's helmet, but it was fast enough to block with its vambraces.

Gresten charged forward and tackled his enemy to the ground. While struggling on the tiles, he held his hand in front of its face and cast another Fireball spell. The demon yelled as its face was engulfed in flames. It writhed in pain, not noticing as the prince climbed to his feet. Gresten slashed the blackguard's throat with his blade.

The prince's side was bloody, so he sat on the floor and used his Healing Hands spell to mend his wound. He needed to be more careful. Perhaps he was being more overconfident than he realised. He should lean inside and check his exit surroundings before throwing himself into a painting portal next time. What if the portal dropped him from the roof?

Gresten continued to search this next floor, entering through a series of different paintings, and winding up at various points throughout the castle. He entered a bedroom and exited from the armoury. He entered a gallery and exited in a broom cupboard. It was more of a maze than Asmuth Swamp. Along the way, the prince killed half a dozen more blackguards. The prince knew that if he had come here when he first planned he would certainly be dead.

Gresten climbed through another portrait and emerged on the fifth floor in a long hallway. He looked to his right and could see a large doorway at the far side. This was the door he sought. This was where Germund had said that Za'gerath was waiting. It now occurred to Gresten that Germund could have been lying to him again to hamper his progress once more.

"If you're wondering whether I was lying, I was not," came Germund's voice as he climbed through the portrait behind Gresten.

"How did you know I was thinking that?" asked Gresten.

"I would have been wondering the same thing."

Gresten and Germund walked down the corridor, coming within feet of the door.

Gresten turned to his brother. "Will you come with me?" he asked.

"I will be of no use," said Germund, "only a

distraction."

"In case I do not return, I have an important question to ask you," said Gresten.

"Yes?"

"Why did our father separate us? Why did he send me with our mother and keep you here?"

"During the plague, Father made a deal with the demon, Za'temnah, to be granted the power of turning stone into gold. With each usage of this power, it sapped a little of his soul. Once he lost half his soul, Za'temnah took our father's body for his own...thus, Za'gerath. He knew it was a possibility that this would be his greatest mistake and damn the entire city, so he kept you and our mother away as a failsafe. If he passed naturally, I could take over here. If we all died in the city, you would survive there, and his bloodline would go on."

"I think that answer distresses me more than if I had continued to not know. We were separated because of his own pride when he knew he was making the greatest mistake to ever befall Lochmeria."

Germund shook his head. "Sometimes the answers disappoint us, but at least knowing the truth allows us to move on."

Gresten nodded and reached for the door.

"Good luck, my brother," said Germund, stepping away.

"Thank you, my brother," said Gresten as he pushed the door open.

The prince walked into the room. It was a large chamber stretching back to the edge of the castle. A small staircase separated the final quarter of the room from the main chamber. The staircase led to the balcony, which gave a magnificent view of the city and the kingdom beyond the walls. Standing at the centre of the balcony, facing the prince, was Za'gerath. The entity that wore his father like a shell.

Za'gerath wore ornate golden armour and a silvery cape. His long blonde hair was tied back in a ponytail and his beard was shaved into a goatee with a moustache. He walked down the staircase towards Gresten and cast his cape aside. Strapped to his waist was a sword with a golden handle and silvery blade that turned blue as it approached the tip. The sword radiated a cold glow.

Gresten walked to the centre of the room holding Zell in his left hand and with his right hand by his side, ready to cast any spells he would need. Za'gerath circled Gresten, not coming within twenty feet of him. He didn't utter a single word, he merely walked around for a full minute.

Za'gerath stopped pacing suddenly and spoke with Gresten's father's voice. "I have watched as you killed my best generals. I wasn't sure that you would last after you were defeated by the Bridge Guardian in your first fight."

Gresten didn't respond, but he maintained eye contact with Za'gerath.

"You would make a fine demon, my son. You could serve me as my next general. I have no doubt that you would be more powerful than any that have come before you, even more powerful than Reinhold could have been had you not slain him so valiantly. What do you say, my boy?"

"I am not your son. I am not your boy. You are wearing my father's corpse like a suit of armour. You have destroyed the fairest city in all of the lands and brought ruin to my kingdom. You will die by my hand."

Za'gerath chuckled. "I am not the monster that you think I am. Do you see how my whelps continue going about their business? Do you see how my miners continue to dig for riches to build this city back? Altburg will be alive once more."

"It's a façade," Gresten stated firmly. "You have taken a beautiful kingdom and hollowed it out. You are ruin, you are destruction. I will have no part of it."

"Let it be known that I gave you a chance," said Za'gerath with a devious smile.

The demon charged towards Gresten with the speed of lightning and Gresten raised Zell only just in time to block a horizontal strike that would have cut his head clean from his body. Za'gerath's strength was formidable. The demon closed his eyes while locked in a clinch with Gresten and teleported backwards onto the balcony. Gresten stumbled forward, almost losing his balance.

Za'gerath shot a ray of lightning towards Gresten, who dove out of the way too slowly. His left arm was hit, and he dropped Zell to the floor in pain. He quickly cast Healing Hands on his arm and retrieved Zell before charging towards Za'gerath, who stood watching and waiting; he was enjoying this.

"You cannot win," said Za'gerath as he blocked Gresten's thrust with his glowing blue sword. Gresten used his Push spell on Za'gerath's leg. The demon stumbled slightly and Gresten slashed him across the right leg. Zell lit up and seared Za'gerath's leg as it cut, its holy magic burning the usurper from within.

The demon king composed himself and smiled, dodging Gresten's next attack. The two exchanged a flurry of slashes and stabs, neither making much ground. Za'gerath cast more lightning at Gresten, who used his Push to sweep the demon's arm aside and redirect the attack.

Za'gerath kicked Gresten back and the two stood facing each other once again. Gresten with Zell raised and Za'gerath with his own sword held by his side. The demon king began pacing around Gresten once again, watching him closely, his mouth curled into a sinister smile.

Gresten raised his hand quickly and cast a barrage of fireballs at Za'gerath, who dodged them all and charged at Gresten. The demon grabbed him by the throat, but screamed in pain, clutching his hand. He staggered backwards, holding out his hand and staring at it in shock; it was red and blistered. With a single swing, Gresten chopped off Za'gerath's burnt hand, and the demon king stumbled backwards, falling onto the floor.

"What have you done?" spat Za'gerath, his voice filled with nothing but pure, seething malice.

Gresten realised what had happened. "A blessing from Saint Rudolph. The True One granted me protection from you. You cannot touch me with your demonic flesh."

"I do not need to touch you to kill you, you cretin."

Za'gerath slashed at Gresten with his sword held in his remaining hand, but the prince blocked each strike. Gresten used his Push spell repeatedly and forced Za'gerath up the stairs, to the edge of the balcony.

The demon king stood up, furious and

dishevelled, and struck once more. Gresten parried the attack, forcing Za'gerath's hand aside. He cut off the demon's remaining hand, and then a swift slash that cleaved through the demon's neck decapitated him. Gresten's father's body collapsed to the floor.

The prince stepped backwards as a black cloud of smoke emerged from King Gerath's open neck, and Za'temnah himself appeared before Gresten. He was a pathetic figure. He didn't look too dissimilar to a frail old man, save for the dark green skin, glowing orange eyes and two curled horns atop his head. He was ugly, he was not a king.

Za'temnah fell to his knees and spoke in a weak, croaky voice. "Spare me, Prince Gresten. I beg of you. Allow me to return to my own domain and I will never set foot in the Lochmeria again. I will banish myself from the entirety of the Outer World."

"No," uttered Gresten as he plunged his sword into the demon's chest before drawing it back out. He swung Zell with all of his might, bringing the enchanted blade round in a wide arc and decapitated the demon's true form, ending his life for good.

Gresten kicked Za'temnah's body aside and knelt beside the remains of King Gerath. The prince prayed to the True One for his father. He prayed that whatever was left of him would reach the Inner World and be at peace, just as he had done for Reinhold. He did not know whether there was anything left of his father remaining while he fought Za'gerath, but he hoped that there was a trace of the true king holding the demon back to protect his son.

"It is done," said Germund, walking into the room.

"It is," said Gresten, turning to face his brother.

Germund walked up the stairs to stand beside Gresten. He took off Hurm's mask and threw it over the edge of the balcony. Seeing his brother's face for the first time was like looking in a mirror, except that mirror made him look paler and somewhat gaunt.

"I hated wearing that," said Germund.

"Was it tied to your curse?" asked Gresten.

"It *was* my curse. Father had it made for me when he could feel his sanity slipping. It was enchanted by Lady Silke of the swamp. It kept me both safe from the biggest threats but at the cost of being bound to the city. Now I'm free to leave."

"Will you?"

"No," said Germund, shaking his head slowly. "I will stay and cleanse the city of the tens of thousands of demons that remain. There are other greater demons that must be dealt with too before I can say my job here is done."

Gresten laughed. "How many greater demons did you not tell me about?"

Germund shook his head, more flippantly than before. "It does not matter. I will deal with them. I can navigate this city like no other after all these years, so who better?"

Gresten embraced his brother, who embraced him back.

"None better," said Gresten, releasing him. "But I will not have you do it alone. I cannot sit idly by while the kingdom is still in turmoil. Once we reclaim the city, the rest of the kingdom must follow."

Germund nodded. "I can't thank you enough, Gresten. I told you that I did not believe you could do it, but I should have had faith."

"All is well, Germund. You gave me the drive to break free of the prison. That was truly the start of my journey."

"Think nothing of it. It was my duty and honour to restore your freedom."

There was one pressing issue on Gresten's mind. "Before we begin, I have a task to attend to first. I promised a young priestess that I would see to it that she was returned home to Warth. I will make good on that promise, but it cannot be today."

"Then we had best work fast," said Germund. "It is a long journey to Warth, but a good opportunity to spread word of our success along the way."

Gresten nodded silently and the two brothers turned to look at the city. In spite of what had become of Altburg, it was still magnificent. The twin princes were determined that it would one day be restored to the shining beacon of the kingdom and their ancestors' legacy would be restored.

Epilogue

Gresten and Germund ascended the winding staircase of the ancient bell tower with conviction. They were battered and bloody, having fought their way to the top through the few demons remaining in the grand city of Altburg, but there was one final task before they could rest. They must slay the former ringer of the bell, the Tower Sentinel.

"We're almost there, brother," said Prince Gresten, his golden hair and silvery armour shining in the evening sun that crept through the narrow tower windows.

"At last," replied Prince Germund. He had his hood up, leaving his face cloaked in shadow and his leather armour kept him nimbler than his brother. "I will wait for an opening once you have him sufficiently distracted."

Gresten nodded. "Good luck, Germund," he

said, clapping his brother on the arm.

"And to you as well," replied the shadowed prince as he climbed through one of the windows and began pulling himself up the tower by his fingertips. It was an impressive skill that Gresten still could not wrap his head around, even having watched his brother scale countless buildings over the last month.

With the demon king dead, the remaining demons grew more desperate and chaotic, but their numbers were dwindling. At last, there was only a single greater demon left to kill and he awaited them at the top of the tower.

Prince Gresten pushed himself up the stairs, his legs burning as he reached the end of the five-hundred-step journey, emerging in the grand belfry. Despite the state of disrepair in the tower, the bronze bell evoked a majestic wonder.

In front of it, wielding a giant hammer and bearing two upright horns atop its head, stood the towering iron knight. A once proud demon hunter, Sir Steyr fell into despair as the city became more debased and corrupt. Nobody knew the full story, but it took shockingly little time for him to abandon his faith in the True One and forfeit his soul.

The prince drew his enchanted blade and slowly walked towards the stoic Iron Sentinel, looking for a gap in the armour where the demon flesh could be pierced by the mighty Zell. The hidden power of the ruby-encrusted blade had torn apart countless demons, and this one would be no exception.

As if to answer the call to battle against its opponent, the Iron Sentinel's eyes glowed red from the slit in its helmet. It held its hammer high and let out a booming grunt as it stomped towards its opponent.

Gresten planted his feet on the ground, ready for the giant to strike. The large hammer swung, a blur as it ripped through the air, aiming directly for the prince's head. He ducked and charged forward as the swinging hammer's momentum forced the Iron Sentinel to control his weapon before attacking once more.

The prince ran behind his opponent, placing himself directly behind its knee. He held out one of his hands and felt a prayer flow through him. An invisible force burst from the prince's hand, bringing the demonic knight crashing down as the prince narrowly avoided the falling titan.

He jammed his sword through the Iron Sentinel's helmet, but he had only broken the skin underneath before a heavy fist knocked him across the room. The prince hurried to his feet and clutched his side. He knew he had been careless and should bide his time.

Gresten glanced upwards, spying Germund in the wooden rafters that supported the ceiling. He had his hands held out, ready to pounce on the final demon lord of the city once it was in position.

The Iron Sentinel ran at Gresten but thrust his hammer forwards. The prince was knocked back to the wall, winded. The towering figure loomed over him and raised his hammer high. He swung it downwards as the prince rolled aside and avoided being crushed into a fine paste.

He scrambled to his feet and ran towards the spot where Germund was waiting above. The Iron Sentinel took the bait and followed him, then Germund pounced. He leapt onto the giant demon's shoulders and ripped the brute's helmet off. The nimble prince tossed the helmet aside and dropped to the ground, giving Gresten a much clearer shot at finishing off their foe.

Angered by the sneak attack, the Iron Sentinel lunged at Germund, grabbing the prince before he could dodge. Germund pulled a dagger from his waist and jammed it into the demon's wrist, but it did not release him. It held tightly, trying to crush the prince.

Gresten charged forwards and used his Force spell, but the Sentinel braced itself and remained standing. He dropped his sword and clung to the beast's leg, channelling his anger. The Heat spell flowed through the prince's hands and the iron armour of the demon glowed red hot. It finally buckled but held tightly to Germund.

Grabbing Zell from the floor, Gresten thrust the sword into the neck of the Iron Sentinel. The magic of the blade burned the creature from the inside. It let out a roar of pain and fury, but it was too late for the demon. Gresten twisted his sword, tearing the beast's throat, then ripped his blade out as its infernal blood coated the brick floor.

The Iron Sentinel fell to the ground with a thud that shook the tower floor and finally released Prince Germund. The last demon lord of Altburg was dead at last, no longer a threat to the once great city.

"Are you alright?" asked Gresten, helping Germund to his feet.

"I...will be...fine," replied Germund, bent over and struggling to breathe. "And you?"

Gresten fell back and lay on the ground. "Just give me a moment to catch my breath."

"There is no time to rest, future king," said Germund. "Go to Warth and come back quickly so that you can be crowned."

"My first order as king will be to have you imprisoned for insolence. My old cell was rather uncomfortable, I shall make sure that it is saved for you."

"I shall bend the bars and climb down," said Germund. "It would not be the first time I have done the latter part of that plan."

The twin princes began to laugh. Slowly at first and then hysterically seconds later. They had finally brought an end to over two decades of the creeping demonic clutches over their fair city and their kingdom.

Gresten stood up and walked over to the rope that hung from the ceiling. He pulled hard and rang the bell. It clanged loudly and spread its beautiful toll throughout Altburg, telling the survivors and the soldiers that they had finally won and telling the last of the demons that they should be fearful.

The twins walked down from the tower, not realising how exhausted they were. Their victory had given them a second wind and they must spread the good news to Saint Rudolph in his cathedral. If anybody could circulate it quickly, it was him.

*

Gresten bid farewell to Germund just past the city gates. Germund, now free from his curse, could step through the gate, but he walked back into the city past the bodies of the many demon whelps that the brothers had slain moments before.

The future king strode down the road towards the field he had left Hilda in. He hopped over the fence and found that his horse was nowhere to be seen. Gresten walked to the far side of the field and saw a young woman feeding Hilda an apple beside a stable.

Maiden Edith saw Gresten approaching and ran to embrace him. He held her tightly for a moment, before letting her go.

"You've returned?" she asked. "All is well in Altburg?"

"I have returned," beamed Gresten. "The last of the demon lords is dead, but there are still lingering fiends that must be killed. My brother will handle that and send word to the loyal that they may now return."

"And I can return to Warth?" asked Maiden Edith.

"Yes. I promised you that I would see to it that you were returned home safe if you waited for me. I want to make good on that promise."

Maiden Edith smiled up at Gresten. "I would like that very much."

Gresten walked over to his horse and stroked her mane. She nuzzled her long face against him, having clearly missed him.

"I'm glad you're safe, girl," said Gresten. "I hope the wait wasn't too long."

Hilda snorted and the two humans laughed.

"We would have liked for you to visit more during the last month," said Edith, "but we kept each other good company. There is nothing for you to worry about."

"I was not worried."

"I'm glad that you trust me so."

"Gather your things, then hop on Hilda. I don't mind walking," said Gresten.

"We don't have to leave straight away, do we?" asked the priestess.

"Maiden Edith, don't you want to return home?"

"I don't think we need the formalities any longer, Prince Gresten. You can call me Edith."

"Edith, don't you want to return home?"

"I would like to see home again, but will you take me to the Isle of Green first?" asked Edith. "You spoke very fondly of it when we first met, and you can spread the good news about Za'gerath's demise."

"It's the opposite direction from Warth, but if that's what you want, I'm happy to take that detour," said Gresten with surprise. "It shouldn't add more than a week to the journey."

"That is what I want," said Edith with a nod.

The young priestess went inside to gather her possessions while Gresten sat on the ground, watching Hilda chew on the grass beside him. He finally felt truly at peace.

Edith returned within a few minutes and climbed atop Hilda. Gresten opened the gate and they all walked over to the road.

The road southwest was long, but a pleasant route. Gresten was pleased that he was returning to the Isle of Green at all, never mind with good news. He was hopeful for the future of Altburg and the future of all Lochmeria.

When he returned, he would receive his coronation and become the new king. He was determined to take this dark age in this hollowed-out kingdom and lay the foundations for a new era of prosperity. The suffering was over.

Printed in Dunstable, United Kingdom